A
WITCH
AWAKENS

The Story

of

Scarlett Gardner

S D C FORSTER

Dedicated to the strong young women of the world.

That's all of you.

"*My name is Scarlett and I have a secret.
I don't know if it's harder to keep or to tell.
I'm not sure my friends would understand, let alone the rest of the world.
I feel alone.*

I think I'm the only one."

CHAPTER
I

THE CLOCK TICKED around to eight. We'd be closing soon. I could hear Esther, the tour guide, doing her "fast track" circuit, so I knew I wouldn't have long to go before I could go home. The last group of guests was in the Ancient Artefacts wing of the museum. I'm sure they were gazing at the antique coins, musing about their origins, and imagining what kind of person would have had them and what they might have bought.

The end of the day was so quiet, lightly littered with footsteps and chatter which grew fainter as closing time approached. As soon as the last guest had exited, I could start my evening ritual. Part of my job was helping to tidy up at the end of the night, having taken tickets throughout the day. I also liked to meander through the exhibits, connecting with the objects, absorbing their ancient stories.

The main entrance door clacked shut, and I heard Esther locking the exits. Removing my name badge, I looked down at it and wiped it clean. An earlier job sorting supplies in the back room had left it dusty. I slowly ran my finger across the gold coloured surface.

Scarlett Gardner—STAFF

I couldn't count the number of these name tags I'd lost over the four years working at the company. I started at our sister museum in Leeds near the university but, as with many of these "holiday jobs," it became full-time after graduation and I transferred down to London. Jackie, my new manager who had already supplied me with three replacements, joked I should just have my name tag tattooed on instead. She said it would be cheaper in the long run.

Slipping the badge into my pocket, I began to make my way around the exhibitions. I straightened out signs, picked up discarded ticket stubs and generally neatened the public areas so that the cleaning crew could do their job more easily. Nearly every rubbish bin I passed had carefully placed paper cups either on top of, or next to, them. Why? Did visitors to London's Museum of Art and Archaeology have trouble disposing paper cups? Clutching a handful of trampled tickets, I looked through the glass display case at pieces of pottery held together on stands. My mind's eye conjured the young women who made them. I envisioned African girls with traditional dress collecting water in the jugs, cooking soups over fire in the pots, and crushing seeds and herbs in the bowls. I wondered how it felt to live so closely connected to nature, eating by the seasons, harvesting with their hands, being at one with the earth. I could see these women as they gathered under a full moon. I was curious about what they shared with each other. If I really concentrated, I could start to feel the heat from the fire they huddled around, hear their laughter and smell the cooking from the pots.

A short, sharp buzz from the phone in my pocket brought me back to reality, reminding me that I probably preferred the twenty-first century complete with internet, instead of waiting months for a messenger in the fifteenth century. I checked my phone. The Whatsapp group message was going nuts. Everyone was in the pub already.

Scar, we're at The George, hurry or you won't get a seat — Rafa

B there sn — Me

I put the phone back in my pocket and continued through the museum doing my tidying-up sweep. I was in a rush, so my stop at the Inca exhibit was brief. The Inca exhibit was my favourite. I always felt welcome there. A warm wave of acceptance emanated from the glass boxes that filled the room, embracing me. I loved looking at the jewellery—sparkling stones embedded in gold and silver. At some point, these jewels were some woman's most important possession. They symbolised power. I knew they would have been cherished and protected. A few deep breaths in this exhibit and I always felt calmer, but this was all I had time for today. I finished checking the rest of the floor, organised the front desk area and grabbed my coat. Double checking my bag for all the necessities—purse, keys, I.D.—I glanced at my phone again and headed for the door.

"Night!" I shouted at Esther, my voice echoing around the halls.

"See you tomorrow, Scar!" She sang, busying herself in the cloakroom.

Stepping outside I sighed, a plume of steam materialising from my mouth. Wrapping my coat around myself tighter, I saw the streets mirroring the night sky after the rain. I listened to the rhythmic sound of my footsteps on the stone pavement and let my mind wander until I saw the street lights ahead were cold. Dull. Lifeless. It was nine o'clock on a November evening and pitch black. The street lights should have been glowing white and bright. Only the faint golden moonlight reflected on the wet cars. Shop fronts usually alive with neon lights were dim and still.

I used to worry about the darkness, about walking alone, my shoes announcing to the world I was here and walking unaccompanied. Anxiety would start to build; my breaths would get shallower and heartbeat faster. The old me would wish those street lights were working, wish the road was bathed in light, wish that someone had called the council to fix the lights the moment they'd broken.

I looked around. It was hard to make out the silhouettes of people, or were they post boxes? Was that noise from the wind or was someone near me? Following me? These were the old thoughts creeping back in, where the sound of the wind would play tricks, mimicking the scuffle of footsteps or the rustle of jackets. I used to panic thinking I was about to be attacked. By this point my heartbeat would have been pounding in my ears.

The pavement started to flicker. Looking down, I saw the reflection of light. Faint at first, bulbs sparked, and, one by one, the lamps fluttered brighter until I looked up and saw all the tall street lights glowing. I looked ahead to the empty road, bare of movement or malice, confident there was no one lurking. Before, I'd have been filled with relief thinking about how fortunate I was that the electricity had finally come on.

Those were the old days when I felt helpless. I didn't worry anymore.

My eighth birthday was when I first noticed something was different. I was different.

The party was at our house. My cake was silver and shaped like a castle with my name at the bottom. I can still see it now, "Happy 8th Birthday, Scarlett." I thought being eight was a big deal. The house was always festively decorated for birthdays. Both my sister, Amber, and I loved all the balloons, streamers, confetti and banners. My parents invited all my aunts and uncles and friends and neighbours. The place was buzzing with people.

I remember that day so clearly even though it was thirteen years ago. The cake was on the kitchen table, half-eaten, surrounded by discarded paper plates and napkins, pale-yellow candles slightly melted and lying to the right. A pile of books lay in a nest of crumpled wrapping paper, exactly the ones I had asked for. The new leotard for my gymnastics practice was hung over the back of the wooden kitchen chair. There was a photo of me in a blue frame behind the cake, my wavy blonde hair falling by my face, freckles prominent from the summer holiday in Cornwall that year. My eyes stood out as usual; they have always been a very vivid green, "like emeralds" people would say back before I knew what an emerald was. Family gatherings consisted of a procession of my relatives gushing about my eyes, "Oh! Look at those gems!" They'd beam at me. I'd try to tell them about schoolwork, my weekends or the book I was reading at the time. But inevitably the response would be, "The boys are going to be hypnotised by those eyes!"

My dad, whose idea of fun has never strayed far from what it was back then, announced his annual session of "birthday tickles." Looking back, it was a very sweet idea—pure and innocent—but I secretly hated it. I remember the intensity, being completely overcome with frustration, yet only being able to scream with joy while loathing every second.

That's when it happened.

During this session of playful tears streaming down my face, I begged my dad to stop. I was powerless to get away, screaming with laughter and a hint of panic. The intensity was too much to bear.

Suddenly, I felt electricity surge in my blood.

BANG!

Every balloon in the house burst.

I felt people in the room freeze. A few guests yelped in surprise, but otherwise we were silent and stock still, including my dad. As we stared at the lifeless rubber remains on the floor, a few people laughed nervously.

I remember thinking it, "I felt like *I* was going to burst."

After that I started to be wary of my emotions becoming too intense. Inevitably something around me would break or crack when they did. Fortunately no one was ever hurt but I worried about the day I wouldn't be so lucky.

At school, the girls mostly left me alone, my head usually buried in a book. Sometimes our school bully was a problem for me. Any girl who made me feel ugly or hated usually ended up getting sick and going home, but Vanessa, a notoriously nasty girl who was overweight and smoked at thirteen, frequently found herself in my face. Despite my avoiding her and her apparent dislike of me, she was always there. She took exception to my green eyes, calling them "snake eyes." Soon that name swept like wildfire through the school. "Scarlett has snake eyes!" She would scream, her pink cheeks puffed out as if she'd just run a marathon.

All the girls would laugh. I hated the laughing. After a quick exit, I would sit on a bench by the library to calm down. The library was foreign territory to those girls.

My one good friend, Alexis, was always there to listen to me vent about Vanessa. She would remind me that at least my sister was being left out of it.

"Think about it, every time she sees you and Amber, she goes for you. You're like a lightning rod. Amber never even gets hit."

"I suppose you're right." I thought about my baby sister, and how I'd hate anyone to treat her like Vanessa treated me. "She'll definitely owe me one when we're older!" I joked.

Sometimes Vanessa would merely sit and snigger with the girls and stare at me. Sometimes she would "accidentally trip," spilling her drink on me. I'd often find myself in the girls' bathroom with Alexis mopping up the orange juice from my white school shirt and dabbing tears from my red face.

I hated Vanessa for a long time, avoiding her in school corridors and using different staircases. Once she developed that nasty rash, she tended to leave everyone alone. Alexis said she deserved it for being so mean. Even though I knew it was wrong to think like that, I couldn't help but agree. I even willed it to get worse. The angry rash engulfed her whole body as the years went by, making her as ugly on the outside as she was on the inside. Eventually she just stopped coming to school, and I found myself wondering if she was ok.

The boys in my year weren't so bad. Mostly they left me alone apart from a few I was friends with. I found them to be much more straight-forward, and usually only had fights among themselves but these would pass like a rain shower and everything would be back to normal. I preferred this to the simmering anger that brewed in the girls, a constant background of distrust towards each other, occasionally boiling over into a fit of tears and name calling. Of course, it would all be resolved with hugs and more crying. Looking back on it all now, it felt so much more important than it really was. I wish I'd known that at the time.

University, on the other hand, was a blast. I studied English at Leeds even though I had no idea where it would go or how I would make money with an English degree. I liked books and stories. Travelling with Gulliver, falling in love with Desdemona, and throwing parties with Gatsby—these were my hobbies and they were my friends. Even exams never felt like exams, they felt like having a discussion with myself about books and writing it down.

There was, however, an incident in my second year that disturbed me for a long time. It was in a nightclub. I was dancing when I felt someone's arms creep around my waist. I wasn't dating anyone at the time and turned to see a stranger getting way too close to me. His other hand started working its way up my leg and under my skirt. Attempting to slip away without a fuss wasn't working. His arm swept around my waist, pulling me in. I couldn't escape his firm grasp.

Pushing myself away as best I could, I shouted at him, "Get off me! Leave me alone!"

He persisted.

I started to panic as I saw nobody could hear me over the deafening speakers. The DJ continued to play tracks while I tried to get the creep away from me, desperate for someone to realise what was happening. My adrenaline was kicking in and, as I took a deep lungful of air ready to scream for him to get off me, the music cut out.

The other dancers stopped and stared in my direction as I let out a piercing cry. Instantly a couple nearby leapt onto my attacker and dragged him off into the arms of security. I announced I was fine and pretended to be for the rest of the night, but it took a long time for me to stop worrying about what could have happened had the music never cut out.

It was because of this incident that I fell in love with combat training. It started with an aerobics class in Body Attack that mixed martial arts with aerobic exercises. I felt so capable, so powerful, and it was intoxicating. I soon moved onto other disciplines, starting with a simple self-defence class before exploring Muay Thai and kick boxing. The rush of adrenaline combined with the dance-like choreography and rhythm of jabs and crosses were addictive. I'd sometimes compete against students from other universities, winning more fights than I lost. My parents said they weren't surprised at my love of fighting; they knew it was always in self defence. Although I had grown up a very calm child who kept to herself, I was never one to run from a problem. They said I would tackle every challenge head on, and so my training seemed to them like the embodiment of this trait. Family jokes revolving around me now ended with shouts of "Don't hurt me, Scar!" and mock cowering. I remember one day, when I was home from university, my dad stopped joking for a minute and became serious.

"Just remember Scar, there are certain things you cannot undo."

"Dad?" I tilted my head to the side and looked at his face. It was unusually serious.

"I remember what your Grandad used to say to me after all his training in the force. You only ever need to neutralise a threat. If you go beyond that, then you're no better than the bad guy." Dad's eyes softened as he remembered his own father.

I reached over and squeezed his hand. "I'll remember. Thanks Dad."

My eighth birthday party was the first time I knew that something wasn't right, that I had a special relationship with my surroundings. External situations echoed my feelings. I was different. Odd things happened around me, but I never really questioned any of it. I grew up thinking I was inexplicably both lucky and cursed. I would fall into puddles. I would forget things and lose them. I would find myself panicking because I wasn't ready for something. But somehow things were always okay. It's not as though I had the answers to quizzes magically in my head, but if I was unprepared for a test, then it would often get postponed.

In my third year at university, I began paying more attention to these strange events. I thought about every funny coincidence, every chance encounter, every "happy accident." My parents would joke that I was a "lucky charm," but I knew I wasn't lucky because the odd things that happened didn't always work out in my favour. Once, as a young teenager, I was out with my mum. We were laden with bags of new school clothes and textbooks when we came across a dog that had been killed in the street. It looked like an Alsatian had been hit by a car and was left smeared on the road so close to me that I could see every harrowing detail. Its eyes struck me first, followed by the rest of the poor creature's final form. It was the worst thing I had ever seen.

I screamed and covered my eyes. "I don't want to see!"

When my mum finally pulled my palms from my face I couldn't see a thing. I was completely blind, which sent my parents into a panic. They rushed me to the hospital only to be given no answers. A specialist was equally speechless. Eventually, the doctors put it down to shock. I put it down to just another one of those quirky things. Three days later my eyesight came back, and everything went back to normal. It would be years later when I realised that I was anything but normal.

Standing in the well-lit street, I smiled and shook my head. It had been a long time since I thought about those days. They had been difficult, and at times painful, but recently things had started to feel less scary. Why, I didn't know. But this wasn't the time to think about that.

I arrived at the pub to the same smells that everyone arrives to: a mixture of freshly spilled drinks on the bar and stale ones stamped into the carpet. No longer does the powerful cloud of tobacco cover these odours. After the smoking ban, every last whiff of drink drunkenly sloshed was exposed. The noise was a mix of cheering from the crowd on TV and people talking loudly over it trying to be heard.

I'm here. Whr r u? — Me

I looked around the room. It was busy for a Wednesday which meant awkwardly weaving through the crowds trying to look for people while trying not to look like someone whose friends had all left.

My hand felt a buzz.

At the back. Big table. Write properly — Rafa

I fought my way past the crowd, heaving my thick winter coat and bag through the last set of human barriers to the back table, dumping them on the chair.

"What's going on?" I asked.

"Scarlett Gardner, at last!" Rafael beamed up at me as he rose from his seat. "Big game's on the TV. I'm going up to the bar. I presume you want the usual." He then turned briefly to smile and say, "And please stop texting like a sixteen-year-old."

"Yeah, yeah, where's my wine?"

"Wine is for grown-ups who write whole words."

I watched him get up and make his way to the bar. Rafael was short for a guy, but he had no trouble with women thanks to his dark brown eyes, hair and olive skin. He was what our friends and I called "short, dark and handsome." He was a good friend I'd made at university and who was now also trying to find his purpose in London. Like a lot of people, Rafael was currently waiting tables. His master was a nearby chain restaurant that served tapas. "The food is terrible and nothing like the real thing, but the owners hired me because I'm 'an authentic Spaniard,' which lends credit to the place." At university, we were in adjacent halls. He studied Sociology and, like me, had no idea what he was going to do after final exams.

"You're SO protective," I once said to him. "You should be a police officer."

"Yeah right." Rafael disagreed.

"Then you could save all the damsels in distress." I insisted.

"You say yourself I believe anything anyone tells me. The bad guys would just tell me it wasn't them! Remember you convinced me the other day that dogs only yawn because they've seen people doing it?"

"You started telling other people!" My sides were hurting by this point.

Rafael had a habit of trying to sound serious, but his eyes would be smiling. It was, in all honesty, a lovely trait in him. He also believed the best in people and always thought there was a valid explanation for someone's shitty behaviour rather than expecting that person to own up to their actions. Rafael would quite vigorously defend people, too. I'd tease him "Just another ridiculous excuse brought to you by Rafael Cuevas García!" like the conversation was sponsored by his optimism. This usually came about after I told him my latest dating tragedy, recounting, for example, how one particular evening's suitor thought it funny to ask if I'd ever thought about breast implants.

"He was probably just making conversation," Rafael helpfully suggested.

"Making the conversation end, more like," I said "He thinks he can make me feel bad about myself? Well he can sit and wait for me to come back from the loo when really I've walked out the back door and cabbed it home." We laughed thinking up scenarios where my loathsome date was still waiting at the table, eyeing up the waitresses' chests and determining whether they, too, should be considering surgery.

"I saw him come into work the other day for dinner, with some girl," Rafael looked like he had some gossip to reveal. His lips were pressed together as if trying to stop the words from racing out of his mouth. "He's put on a lot of weight, you know. He looked like he had a real set of moobs on him!"

"Perfect. He must be so pleased!" I giggled.

Sometimes the nightmare dating life was worth it just for the comedy debriefing sessions with Rafael that followed.

He would try not to collapse in hysterics but every time we had this kind of conversation it just seemed more and more ridiculous. On one occasion, an unexpected guest turned up.

"His girlfriend, you say?"

"Yes. He had a bloody girlfriend!" I admitted, still in disbelief.

"And was she nice?" He teased me, trying to get a reaction.

"I didn't have time to find out actually!" He was always one to make me smile in times of drama. "I was so mortified, but then the fire alarm went off, and we all had to evacuate. I slipped off home while she was busy shouting at him in the street!"

It reminded me of so many other talks we had had at university. Rafael was always there for a cup of tea and a chat, but eventually it just made me question whether I really was bad at dating.

James and Natasha were still sitting across the table watching the TV screen on the wall behind me. I noticed it was a Premier League game, which explained the crowds. Seventy-five minutes gone so far, another fifteen to go plus injury time, and most of these people would leave. James' blue eyes looked grey and tired. He had not long started a new job in the city, and the boss was working him hard by the sound of it. We joked that we didn't know what he did for a living.

"How's the accountancy going, Jim? Are you cooking the books properly?" I smiled.

"I'm not an accountant," grumbled James.

"Stock market not treating you so well today, huh?" Natasha joined in.

"I'm not a trader!"

"Look, I'm sure those shareholders will be pleased you landed the Henderson account." I couldn't help myself sometimes. He was so easy to wind up.

James sighed and rolled his eyes dramatically. He didn't have the energy to kid back today it seemed. He turned his pint glass round in his hand and his attention back to the TV. Being a bit of a grump, we were used to him and ignored any and all sulking. I looked at Natasha who finished a text and put her phone away in her pocket.

"How was work?" Natasha asked.

I shrugged. "Same thing, different day."

"Still thinking of getting a new job?"

"Nah. It's boring and quiet, but there's something about the stuff in there. I love being there. Makes me feel good."

"Hah, okay, Weirdo. I remember the museum field trips at school were the worst." Natasha pulled a face, clearly glad those days were over.

"You were thinking of getting a new job?" James chimed in unexpectedly. I wasn't aware he'd been paying attention.

"Yeah, a while ago. Can't see this going anywhere, but it's okay for now."

James started turning his pint glass around in his hand again, looking up at the TV, but he didn't seem to be watching it. His focus no longer followed the ball on the screen. James was a friend that Rafael, Natasha, and I had just met in the pub one day. I saw this tall guy with dirty blonde hair and glasses approach our table with a beer in his hands. He said his friends had left to go to an eighties bar, which we all agreed sounded like hell on earth, so we invited him to sit with us. He seemed like a nice, normal guy, so when he added me on Facebook, I just started inviting him along to stuff. Plus, he lived pretty close to Natasha and me. We were all in the west of London. Natasha had answered my online advert after my last housemate moved out of our tiny place around the corner from Ladbroke Grove tube station. Rafael was in Kensal Rise, and James lived in Westbourne Park. It's always a risk living with a stranger, although from stories I've heard it's no safer moving in with a friend. I hear it a lot. Best friends decide to live together then they find out that one can't stand the mess left in the kitchen or the other hates a chore chart. Natasha is pretty easy going, though. She's never had a complaint about me, and she likes to help out when things break.

A few nights earlier, the radio had packed up when she was in the shower. She was singing along to a cheesy chart hit that I couldn't stand. When she belted out the key change, I threw my shoe at the bathroom door from my bedroom.

"I'm going to evict you if you don't stop!" I yelled. The music promptly cut out. I worried she had taken the threat of being kicked out seriously, but after a few minutes she emerged from the bathroom, towel wrapped around her and long chestnut hair dripping wet.

"Radio broke. Right at the good bit." Frowning, she padded across to her room, humming the tune, and shut the door.

Rafael came back from the bar with a drink in each hand and a packet of crisps under each arm. Relieved at his initiative, I whipped one away from him hungrily and opened it in half so it lay flat on the table.

"Thanks!" I chewed at him. We continued to sit there, picking away at the crisps and chatting about our days even though nothing particularly interesting had happened to any of us. Rafael had a big table at lunch who spent £200 and tipped him £3.50, Natasha worked at an organic food shop so her stories revolved around overhearing Notting Hill ladies' conversations about the trials of finding a decent nanny, and James, well, James liked to tell us why the goal that was just scored on TV was actually offside. He had clearly started watching the game again.

On the way home, the biting cold encouraged Natasha and me to huddle together, awkwardly manoeuvring around puddles and post boxes. We rounded the corner onto Lancaster Street and climbed the steps up to the porch. As I searched in my bag for the house keys, I heard the motion activated light click on.

"Look." Natasha's forced whisper sounded urgent.

"What?" I wasn't paying attention properly, annoyed at losing track of my keys.

"Did you come home before the pub?"

"No, why?" I continued to rummage through my bag. Things often slid into the broken lining.

Natasha grabbed my arm harder this time. Her voice was louder, and it was shaking. "Scarlett! Look up! The front door's open."

CHAPTER
2

W E STOOD FROZEN for so long the security light clicked off. The biting wind was still swirling around us, making the large, black, outer door creak to and fro as it swung. The door that opened into our flat had clearly been kicked in.

Natasha was gripping my arm tighter. "What do we do?" She whispered. Her voice was shaking.

"Call the police, Tash."

Natasha nodded and gently backed away down the stairs dialling 999 on her mobile. After making sure she was distracted, I slowly crept forward, pushing the heavy front door open, stepping inside and looking through to our flat. I figured if there was anyone here, at least I could practice using my Muay Thai. The communal hallway gave away nothing and was bare except for the odd discarded umbrella. As I inched closer to our flat and into the living room, I could see the chaos. I looked closer. Something wasn't right. Yes, it was a mess but I couldn't see anything beyond that. Not in the living room at least. The light green sofa cushions were askew. Lamps were tipped on their sides. Every book was thrown across the room. I looked to the window to see the curtains had been pulled down from their rail, and the flower vase had been knocked onto the floor. Venturing further into the kitchen, I saw draws of upturned cutlery and smashed plates on the floor. Back in the living room, I noticed the flat screen TV was still there, tipped forward on to its face. Why didn't they take it?

Natasha came rushing in.

"Scar! What are you doing in here? The police are on their way. This isn't safe. We shouldn't be in here!"

"It's okay. There's no one here. They didn't even take anything." This was an attempt to calm her before I moved to go upstairs.

"What are you talking about? Look at this place! Scarlett, please don't go up there!"

"Natasha, stop it. Look, the police will be here soon. Stay outside and wait for them. Tell them whatever they want to know."

I hadn't heard any movement in the flat since we returned and took that as a sign we were alone. We lived in one of those giant old west London houses that had been divided into flats. Ours was especially narrow with three floors. It was also particularly creaky. All the lights were on upstairs, so whoever had broken in must have been in every room. I couldn't figure out why, though. What did they want? Why were they ransacking our place without taking anything?

Something felt wrong.

I edged closer to my room, and I knew this was where they had wanted to go. This was reason they broke into our home. My stomach tightened as I approached. Gently pushing the bedroom door open with my fingertips, I expected it to be ransacked. But when I surveyed my overturned room, nothing had been taken. My curtains had been pulled down, and my mattress was flipped onto the floor, but nothing more.

I suddenly felt weak, and my head began to spin. Backing away from my bedroom door and gripping the banister, I retreated downstairs to see Natasha standing with two police officers. They were just inside the door to our flat; it led straight into what was now our chaotic living room. Natasha was explaining how people don't always make sure the outer door closes behind them. As I creaked down the stairs, one officer turned to me, eyes wide with surprise that someone else was there.

"Who are you?" The older officer asked, flipping her notebook. Ready to write.

I sat on the bottom steps sighing heavily, looking up at her in the doorway to our flat.

Luckily Natasha intervened. "Oh! This is my flatmate, Scarlett Gardner. We came home together."

"You really shouldn't have been upstairs, Miss. We always ask people not to touch anything as it could hinder our investigation." The policewoman's face creased with disappointment. Both officers stepped further into our living room. The younger one peered up the stairs behind me.

"I know. Sorry." I shook my head attempting to clear my foggy, dizzy brain. It didn't work.

Natasha looked scared. "I couldn't stop her. She wanted to see the damage and what might have been stolen." She shrugged. "It didn't look like anyone was still here."

I tried to smile reassuringly. "Don't worry, Tash, doesn't look like they took anything."

She exhaled loudly and rubbed her temples firmly with her fingertips.

I stood up and went over to her, putting my arm around Natasha's shoulders to comfort her. "Maybe they were looking for cash and didn't realise that we're both broke?" I joked with her. "Come on, we'll answer some questions, let these guys look around, and then have a cup of tea. Okay?"

When the police left and we had tidied up a bit, I turned on the TV hoping a bit of background noise would soothe us both. It was two o'clock in the morning, and we were exhausted, but it was easy to tell Natasha wasn't ready to go to her room on her own. She sat clutching her tea thinking furiously about something but wouldn't tell me what. Eventually, I heaved both of our duvets down to the living room, put on a film and suggested we both bunk downstairs on the sofa for the night. Natasha smiled weakly—a small improvement—and we sat together in silence until we fell asleep.

I awoke to the sound of talking coming from the kitchen. The awkward night's sleep had left me with a crick and unable to turn my head properly. Rubbing my neck carefully, I hoisted myself to my feet and started to drag the duvets upstairs. The wall clock read a little after nine in the morning, but I was still tired. Going up to my room made me feel faint, which I put down to needing breakfast. Those crisps at the pub last night didn't exactly count as a square meal.

Downstairs, Natasha hung up the phone. She looked out the window, stirring a cup of tea.

"How're you doing?" I went over to the counter, yawning and still massaging my neck.

"Okay, I guess. I hate that someone's been in here. I called work to say I'm not coming in today. I also rang the landlady to get someone to fix the door." She stopped staring into the garden and turned to face me.

"Good." I chirped sleepily. "I don't have to be at the museum until twelve, so let's have breakfast. I'll make some bacon, and we can have sandwiches. Or do you want eggs?" I was already banging the pots and pans together as I pulled them from the cupboard.

Natasha carried on stirring her tea and went back to gazing out into the garden. I was sure something else was bothering her, but I wasn't about to start interrogating her after the night we'd had. Maybe the smell of a delicious cooked breakfast would help; it always perked me up. I tried to get a sense of what had happened the night before but was drawing a blank. The kitchen radio was on and that cheesy song started playing again.

"That song should be banned." I groaned loudly. "Who came up with that repetitive rubbish? No imagination at all!" I was sure she would respond to my complaint about her favourite song. Nothing. So, I joked, "I should yank the plug out of the socket. Anything's better than that auto tune."

Natasha kept on looking out the window. The song carried on playing.

As I wiped my mouth and clattered my cutlery onto a now empty breakfast plate, I heard a knock on the door. Aware that I was about to answer the door in my pyjamas, I ran my fingers through my hair to neaten up and wiped last night's mascara away from under my eyes. I pulled the broken door open. Our landlady, Ms Birch, was standing in the hallway. She always looked very well put together, and this morning was no exception. Her black skinny jeans and emerald green winter coat made her look very stylish. I secretly hoped I could look half as good when I'm in my sixties. Her long grey hair had streaks of white in it and was neatly swept up into a twist held in place with an ornate pin in the shape of a peacock. I welcomed her in as she reached out her arms to give me a hug.

"Oh Scarlett! Natasha told me what happened. Are you alright?" She squeezed me tightly before releasing me to look around.

"Oh, it's okay. They didn't actually take anything." I tried to quell her concern even though I was worried *why* they didn't take anything.

Ms Birch hugged me briskly again before spinning around. "They really did a number on this door! I've already got someone coming round to fix it. He'll make sure it's positively impenetrable." Her voice always sounded as if she was very slightly singing; it was comforting even in a situation like this. Ms Birch smiled warmly at me and glided into the kitchen to see Natasha. I closed the door into the broken frame as best I could and followed.

"I think we're fine." Natasha reassured her. They were both sat at the kitchen table. "But we need to make sure whoever it was doesn't come back."

"Of course, my dear. Of course. We'll make sure of that."

"Thanks." Natasha gave her a relieved smile.

"Cup of tea, Ms Birch?" I went to put the kettle on.

"Now Scarlett, I told you to call me Ivy."

"Sorry," I blushed. She was so charming. We were lucky to have her as a landlady and I would joke we had clearly hit the renter's jackpot. You hear some real horror stories in London. "Would you like some tea, Ivy?"

"No, dear." She leapt up. "I must be off. Things to do!" She had only been in our flat a few minutes but seemed to be in a rush. Come to think of, she never stayed long.

"Oh, okay. Thanks for coming over to check on us and for sorting the door."

"Don't mention it. Be safe, okay? Let me know if there's anything else you need." She looked at Natasha, adding "Be very sure they didn't take anything, okay? Check the whole house." Then, she promptly swept back out through the living room.

"Ivy's nice, huh? If not a bit eccentric." I commented turning the taps on to wash the breakfast dishes.

"She's the best." Natasha smiled.

At eleven o'clock, I left the house and started to feel much better. By the time I got to work, the dizzy feeling had worn off entirely. Thoughts of who could have broken in were still whirring fruitlessly through my mind. Thankfully, there were still a few minutes before my shift, so I took a walk around the wings of the museum. I scrutinised the events of the night before. Why break in and tear up a place if you weren't going to take anything? I tapped my fingers on the glass of the Inca jewellery exhibit looking at the gold necklaces embedded with gemstones of all different colours. Surely, you don't break into someone's house hoping to find piles of cash? I walked around the cabinet to get a closer look. The gold glinted in the specially placed spotlights; it was mesmerising. Who was the real target? Me or Natasha? Was someone trying to scare us? We had no enemies to speak of, or at least none that were obvious.

As I looked at the glinting jewels, my mind suddenly flashed white. I lost my balance. Taking a second to steady myself, I looked harder at the stones. They were beautiful tiger eye stones, with bands of gold undulating across them. Looking deeper, I tried to clear my mind, but again it sparked brightly, forcing me to lean my weight against the glass cabinet. This time, I saw something: a figure dressed in black. It was hard to make out who it was, but I could see they were in our flat.

I closed my eyes and took a breath, trying to clear the picture. The figure was too tall and broad to be a woman. He went upstairs with one arm awkwardly bent and pressed against his hip, there was something in his pocket that was important. I closed my eyes tighter, my hands pressing flat against the glass. He was heading towards my room. What was in his hand?

The sudden arrival of tourists pouring through the doors brought me back to myself in the museum with a jolt, the mental picture frustratingly dissolving just as the man was poised to go into my room. I wiped the sweat from my forehead. I knew that I had just seen the man who broke into our home. I also knew other people didn't experience this kind of thing. No one had ever mentioned having visions before, and I never wanted to enquire in case people started asking questions I couldn't answer or thought I was crazy. But I was sure people didn't experience what had just happened to me. The flashes had reminded me of something, and I had a vague memory that it had happened before when Amber and I were younger.

At fourteen-years-old, Amber was hit by a car. Since it wasn't going that fast, she only needed a few stitches on her elbows. The driver, however, had left her in the road crying and covered in bloody scrapes. When I had heard the story of what happened, I was furious. Amber tried to convince me she was okay, showing me her injuries all sewed up. But the rage was already bubbling up under my skin. I stormed outside, not really expecting the car to be around still, but I just wanted to be in the place where it happened.

That's when I saw it. First, the blinding white flash. Then, the burgundy sports car screeching off and my sister's cries echoing in my head. I somehow knew the license plate. I saw it clear as day. I told Amber to memorise it and to tell the police she suddenly remembered it. They found the guy with a dent in his bonnet and no explanation for how it got there. I guess I forgot because no one ever knew I told Amber the plate number, and she was too young to ask questions.

Well, it had happened again, except this time someone had put something in my room.

The rest of the day passed slowly. The early evening inched in as I continued to sell tickets and hand out maps of the museum. I ate my late lunch in the small café. I usually brought a sandwich in but, with the turmoil of the night before, I had forgotten to make anything. I sat down with my tray on the corner table and got out my phone.

Did Tash tell u wat happnd? — Me

I messaged Rafael. He was on the closing shift so wouldn't be at work yet. I didn't know how much I should tell him. Maybe just that someone broke in or that I thought they did it to hide something in my room? But then how would I explain it? It was hard to keep things from him but I also didn't want him to think I was crazy.

James told me, are you okay? — Rafa

Natasha must have told James. I decided to keep things vague. I had too much on my mind to worry about what Rafael thought of my weird mind trips.

Yeh, freaked bt all gud x — Me

Ok well if you need anything just message me. Are you about this weekend? — Rafa

Nope, wkend off. Going 2 c my folks 2moro. Chk in on Tash 4 me? — Me

Will do. Let me know if there's anything else. I worry about you! — Rafa

I polished off my overpriced coronation chicken sandwich, wiped my mouth with the napkin and drained the last of my diet coke before taking the tray to the bin. The late crowd who liked a lazy morning and a leisurely lunch started arriving. I figured I should get back to the front desk. The image of the man in our flat plagued me for the rest of the day.

At home, every bit of evidence that someone had broken in the night before had been completely eradicated. The flat had a new door with a new lock. Natasha had left the key with a neighbour. Every book, lamp and cushion was back in its proper spot. In fact, the whole place looked cleaner than before. Natasha must have been busy, but not too busy to leave me a note saying she was staying at a friend's house tonight. She was thoughtful like that.

I dumped my bag on the sofa and took a deep breath, trying to recreate my vision, but it was faint and blurry. Stepping closer to the stairs it seemed obvious what I needed to do. But I became more confused with each pace towards my room. What was I doing? I got to the top and looked along past Natasha's room to mine. The door was open, and the curtains had been re-hung. My hands fiddled anxiously with the buttons on my blouse as I got closer. When I got there, my room looked exactly like it always had. What was I worried about? There was no sign someone had been rooting through my things. All my books were still here. My laptop and hair straighteners were in their usual places. I had a feeling I was forgetting something, but I was more relieved that it looked as if we could put this whole horrible incident behind us. From now on, we'd make sure the outer door was always closed properly. With the stronger flat door, nothing like this should ever happen again. Reassured, I went back downstairs to make dinner and read awhile. Later that night I slept a deep dreamless sleep.

On Saturday morning, the sun rose and I fell in love with London all over again. The tourists hustled, and the locals bustled while the streets smelled of coffee and croissants. Sunny December mornings always had this effect on people, especially on the weekends. This day was no exception. With my overnight bag on my arm and cold air in my lungs, I locked up the flat and headed down the stoop to the tube station. My iPod was playing loudly and I practically skipped my way to Paddington Train Station. The extortionate ticket prices weren't even angering me as they usually did, and I settled down on the ten fifty-eight to Bristol Temple Meads. It took under two hours to get there. I was always armed with a magazine, but the passing countryside often distracted me.

Alternating fields of yellow with rolling hills of green dotted with fluffy white. I find simply sitting and letting thoughts flow through my head to be very therapeutic. The telephone poles were passing rhythmically now, and the grassy backdrop was a welcome change to the usual London "pavement grey." The sun was still shining brightly, making the winter sky a deep cobalt blue and warming up the inside of the train carriage. I took my coat and scarf off and placed them on the next seat hoping no one would sit next to me. The carriage looked empty enough as I took a second to glance up and down the aisle.

I noticed a man making his way through the aisle. His body was turned slightly sideways because he was larger than most. His black windbreaker was noisily brushing up against people's seats. Something stirred in me. The swishing sound got louder as he eventually passed. I turned my head to look out the window. What was I forgetting? That man looked familiar.

As the train rolled into the old, familiar station in Bristol, I got the expected pang of nostalgia. Remembering the nights as a teenager going to nearby towns dressed to the nines to sneak in for drinks, I smiled. Now, I'm nearly always in jeans and Converse at the pub. Surely, an unequivocal sign of underage drinking is the height of the stilettos and how many layers of mascara a girl is wearing?

The smell wafting from the Cornish pasty vendor pierced me as if it were my own mum's home cooking. It nudged my memories about coming back after those heavy nights out and sinking my teeth into a pasty. I felt like the happiest person on earth.

The ticket machine ate up my return ticket, spat it back out and welcomed me home. I turned to drag my bag through before it abruptly slammed shut again. Mum was waiting where she usually did: outside in the car. I put my things in the boot and plonked myself on the seat next to her. She was wearing her new driving glasses that she'd reluctantly agreed to. The pink top I'd bought her for her birthday made her look trendier than usual.

"Hello darling." She smiled. "How was the train ride?"

"Oh, you know, the usual. Weather's nice, isn't it? I like the west country in the sunshine. I didn't eat on the train, though. Are we having lunch at home?"

"Yes, don't worry. Your dad is on the case. I sent him off to Waitrose earlier to get some fancy cheese and ham and that bread you like."

"Thanks, Mum." I watched her as she peered over the steering wheel trying to navigate her way out the car park. It was a good twenty-minute drive to the house so I told her about work, about my friends and about how I was managing to save money. I stayed off the subject of the break-in because it would only worry her.

"Any young men on the horizon?" Mum liked to ask this question without looking directly at me because the sheer amount of hope she held for the answer might show on her face.

"No one yet, Mum. These apps are making it hard to know if you really want to meet someone. You just get a picture and a crap chat-up line."

"Sounds the same as meeting someone in a bar, except you don't have to get all dressed up. Which picture have you put up? Maybe it's giving the wrong impression?" She continued to diligently watch the road ahead.

"The picture's fine, Mum. If he doesn't like me in my Halloween skeleton costume, then I don't want to know him." I said this to wind her up, and it worked perfectly.

We went on to talk about Amber and how she was getting on at Loughborough. It felt odd that my little sister was at university. Actually, it felt *old* to have my little sister at university. Only a couple of years ago she was doing her GCSE's, and I was leaving home to explore a life of unsupervised drinking. She was having a good time, though, and enjoying her sports scholarship. Unlike Mum, I knew exactly what she was up to because she was eighteen and everything she did got tagged on Facebook.

We pulled up to the house and the front door opened to reveal Dad holding back the dog. Jet, the black Labrador, wasn't trusted out on his own, he had as much enthusiasm for escaping as a convict on death row.

"Let him go, Dad. He's not going to run off!" I collected my bag and slammed the car boot shut.

"We've lost him twice this week! I'm not risking it." Dad was pulled forward by Jet's collar with every excited jump.

I thought it best to get inside as soon as possible before someone's shoulder got dislocated. I gave Dad a hug and a kiss on the cheek. "I promise to take Jet for a walk after lunch. Maybe I can tire him out a bit." Jet jumped up at me like I had bacon in my pockets. I gave him a cuddle and a scratch behind the ears.

After putting my bag away in my room, I went downstairs to have lunch. Dad and I had the same conversation as I had in the car with Mum detailing my life since I last saw them.

I always enjoyed seeing my dad when I went home. I didn't talk to him on the phone as much as I did with Mum, plus he was always much better value in person. Dad was always one for physical comedy, preferring to take the "fake elevator down" over some clever wordplay, but I loved this about him. What you saw was what you got with Dad. He had worked all his life as a postman, giving him a good sense of direction and killer calves. Well, I should really say one killer calf and one prosthetic one. Dad had lost his right leg in a motorcycle accident years ago when I was little, and Amber wasn't even born yet. Needless to say, Mum had always warned him about how dangerous motorcycles were, but he loved the feeling he got from riding. It was liberating. Exhilarating. *It made him feel alive.* But one rainy day, he decided to get out on the bike, and, in a split-second, his life changed. Dad describes it as one of the worst moments of his life. He thought he was going to die when that lorry collided with him. Now, he considers himself lucky, being spared and getting to live the rest of his life as normal. More or less. I remember going to visit him in the hospital, but his demeanour was still so upbeat it never really clicked that anything bad had happened. The insurance helped cover the new leg and the mortgage payments until he was literally back on his feet. The post office didn't expect him to return to work, but typically Dad made a joke out of it. "I'm half machine now. I'll do my rounds twice as fast!" I loved his bravery. He saw the best in every situation. It was something he'd inherited from his own dad. Grandad had been a police officer with the Avon and Somerset Constabulary until he passed away. Those strong morals had been passed down to Dad, and now he was doing the same. He's always been a role model to Amber and me.

We got to know all our neighbours so well because Dad was the local postie. We didn't even mind always getting our mail last when he finished his rounds. During the school holidays when we were little, Amber and I would ride along on our bikes beside him until he finished our street and moved on. We watched him work and asked him questions. "What if you can't read the address? What if there's a big dog? But you like dogs, don't you, Dad? What if there isn't a stamp?" The man never lost his patience. In fact, I think he liked the company, answering me every time by referencing the Post Office manual. He took his job seriously and worked hard even though a lot of people thought it was easy.

The front door clicked shut behind me. Grey clouds began to draw across the sky like a curtain. The short winter's day would soon be over. Wrapped up in my warm hiking gear and wellies, I was feeling the sharp cold air only on my face. It felt good to breathe it in. I could feel it all the way down into my chest as I strode up the hill to the spot where I liked to stop and let Jet run about. He was very good with me. Despite a few manic laps around the field, he would always return to potter about at my feet as I rested on the bench admiring the view. I came here to sit, studying the way the land rolled around the hillside, noticing the blurs of dirty white fluff on the farms, and watching the birds play tag in the sky.

Despite the cold weather, it had yet to snow this year, but forecasters were saying it was imminent. I was excited because snow is easily the best thing about Christmas. Some of the trees were stubbornly holding onto their greenery; others had long since given up in favour of waiting for the weather to improve. Then, they would sprout a whole new world of emerald, and the fertile scene would burst back to life.

I sat on the bench, taking in the beauty and peacefulness of the landscape. Jet was tired of running and came to lay a few feet away from me. My warm jacket and special socks meant I could sit for ages without getting cold and, as I looked at the lavish view in front of me, my mind began to wander.

About two seconds later, it hit me. The man in black! That's what was bugging me on the train. I remember it all now! Why didn't I check my room when I got home last night? I was so intent on it. Why had I thought about nothing else at work the rest of the day only to go home and completely forget? I couldn't understand it. I made a note in my phone, a reminder to alert me after I get back to the flat to look for anything hidden in my room. I was starting to have suspicions, not about the form of what might have been left there but, more importantly, its purpose. I took a deep breath of cold air and blew it out in a puff of steam. I felt annoyed at myself for forgetting while I was still at home and able to search for it. What good was remembering while I was miles away in Bristol? My mind raced again through the various theories I had thought of the day before. I wondered whether I could make myself see something else about that night—something that might even tell me who the man was. But I struggled to summon up any images. I concentrated hard, eyes focused on the neon yellow tennis ball that Jet had brought to me. I drew even, controlled breaths. I cleared my mind but feelings of annoyance and anger at myself still lingered. Focusing on the ball, I attempted to crystallise the vision that had come so easily into my head at the museum. I desperately tried to force my brain to do something. Anything.

The ball started to move.

I carried on directing all my energy and attention on it. I felt that I could do something but until it happened, I wasn't sure what it was. All I could think of was the direct line between my eyes and the yellow fuzz covering the slightly chewed tennis ball. I stared as it wobbled, then bobbed up and down. Eventually, the ball was floating a foot up in the air. A small part of me couldn't believe what was happening, but I kept focusing on the ball. As I did, it rose higher and higher. I looked up to the sky as Jet's favourite toy was now fifteen-feet high, suspended in a backdrop of grey clouds. I was astounded. I'd never seen anyone else do this before. I didn't think anyone else could.

Jet began to bark up at his favourite toy poised high above his head. As my eyes shot down to see what the commotion was, the tennis ball came plummeting down. It bounced on the grass and caused the dog to bound with joy, tearing towards it before running away with his prize.

I sat on the bench feeling simultaneously exhausted and exhilarated. My body wanted to dance with excitement but was too tired to get up. I knew exactly what had just happened. I had made something move just by looking at it. Not only that, but I had lifted it fifteen feet straight up in the air. I couldn't wait to try it again, but I had been so distracted, I didn't notice the sun had dipped well below the horizon, and the clouds were darkening. Mum would be worrying about me. After a few minutes to regain my strength, I rose to my feet and rubbed my cold hands together, whistled for Jet who enthusiastically came running over, re-attached his lead and headed for home.

I was happy. I felt an important part of me had clicked into place.

CHAPTER
3

L OOKING OUT THE window at the rain violently firing into the pavement, the glorious winter sunshine from the weekend seemed a distant memory. My hair was still wet from the thirty second sprint from Ladbroke Grove tube station to my front door, and I sniffed and rubbed my nose with my sleeve as I waited for the kettle to boil. Leaning my hips forward against the kitchen sink, I looked at the security camera facing the entrance to the back door. There was an identical gadget on the front door, too. Rafael had persuaded us to let him install them for safety. After he turned up with the equipment already paid for, who were we to say no? Ms Birch thought it was a great idea and insisted on paying Rafael for his work. If we had another break-in, we'd catch the perpetrator on camera and have something tangible for the police, although I hated the thought of it happening again.

The kettle began to whistle, and I poured the boiling water into our two favourite mugs. Natasha was on the sofa. She had yet to go outside and was romanticising the sound of the rain.

"Doesn't it relax you?" She was distractedly turning the page of her book.

"Not when I'm still wet, no." I sniffed again and passed her a cup of milky tea, keeping a hold of mine a bit longer to warm my hands.

"It's not my fault you forgot your umbrella."

She had a point. I sank down into the sofa and thought about the lovely weekend at my parents' house in the country. It was always so nice to go home. Even though as a kid I thought home was nothing special, now it's a place of comfort and security, of provision and guidance. As I sat in our cold little flat, I thought about visiting home more—not just in a couple of weeks for Christmas but throughout the new year. This seemed like it would be a good New Year's resolution. I sipped my tea and started thinking about getting changed into drier clothes when my phone made an odd sound.

> *Reminder: Check your room for something left there during the break-in! Ask Tash to help!*

I looked at the notification on the screen. While I remembered putting this message into my phone, I didn't know why it was so important. Surely, the police were on the case as to who broke in. And they admitted there was very little evidence to go on, so why did I think I could solve the mystery?

"Um, Tash? Could you give me a hand with something?"

Natasha looked up from her book, her eyebrows raised.

"You know when that guy broke in? Don't think I'm crazy or anything, but I think he left something in my room that's been making me feel a bit funny. Could you help me root about? It's probably nothing, but I just have a hunch."

"You think he left something weird in there? Feeling funny? In what way?"

"I don't know." I shrugged. "Please, will you help me?" I looked over at her to see if she was still reading her book, but she was already getting to her feet. Fortunately, she was not the judgemental type.

Back in my room, I saw the number of wrappers left lying about on my desk from before the weekend and started to tidy up, sifting through the receipts I needed and the ones I could throw in the bin. Then, I noticed the laundry hamper was full and went to take it downstairs to the washing machine in the kitchen.

"Where are you going?" Natasha asked as she rolled out the drawers from under my bed and rifled through the spare linen.

"To do some laundry. What are you looking for?"

"But you just . . . ?" Natasha's eyes widened before shaking her head at me. "Never mind. Go do your laundry." She mumbled as I walked out of the room and down the creaky stairs.

I heard her continue to open drawers and wardrobe doors, wondering if I took something of Natasha's and forgot to return it. As I stuffed my week's-worth of work blouses into the machine, I heard loud scraping as if furniture was being moved about upstairs. I sat back down in the living room to my cup of tea. The sound of watery whirring came from the kitchen as Natasha marched down the stairs and went straight out the front door into the street. Without her coat. It was still raining, so I wondered what she would possibly need to do outside, but she reappeared a few minutes later, dripping wet. I heard the loud exhaust of a passing lorry driving off.

"What's the matter with you? You're soaked!" I said.

Natasha looked at me with a confused smile before waving me away. "Nothing, I just forgot something I left outside when I came home last night. No big deal. Is your washing on?"

"Yeah, although with this weather, I'll be hanging it all on the radiators again." I looked back outside to the grey skies and listened to the pattering on the windowsill. Maybe rain *was* kind of romantic.

I awoke that night to the sound of people knocking over the bins outside. This often happened when patrons of the local pub stumbled their way to the nearest stop for the night bus. Always one to look on the bright side, my dad said that, when this happens, I should feel bad for the people who live next to the bus stop. It made me smile because he always had a great sense of perspective. Unfortunately, it was always hard to get back to sleep after this drunken alarm clock. Rolling onto my side, I pulled the duvet up to my neck and hugged the hot water bottle. It got chilly at night, and as I waited for my bed to warm up I saw that my desk drawer was open. Natasha must have left it like that earlier. I debated whether to brace myself against the cold room, get up and close it, or to stay in my warm cocoon. I looked at the drawer, annoyed. I was so comfy, but this gaping drawer was going to irritate me and keep me awake. I stared severely at the drawer. My eyes narrowed. That bloody drawer. I didn't want to get up, but I wanted the damned thing to close.

THWACK!

I nearly jumped out of my warm bed. The drawer slammed shut right in front of me. I looked around the room—not exactly sure what I'd see—only to confirm that I was completely alone. I lay motionless for a moment, thinking how familiar this was. The noise had startled me because I didn't expect it, but the drawer shutting seemed less surprising. That's when I remembered Jet's tennis ball. The thing lifted into the air simply because that's what I wanted it to do. The drawer in my desk had shut exactly like I wanted it to! I was excited. Thoughts and feelings started coming back to me, and I got the impression that I had already contemplated this a great deal. Smiling, I lay back in bed to explore these new memories. I didn't mind so much being woken up anymore. Then, the figure in black moving through the hallway of our flat re-emerged in the back of my brain. Instinctively, I knew Natasha had found something in my room. She must have disposed of it outside. What had it been? How did she know what it was, and why she didn't tell me about it?

I looked at my alarm clock. It wasn't even three in the morning yet, but this was too important. I braced for the cold. Still clutching my hot water bottle, I crept into Natasha's room to sit on the edge of her bed. She groaned as I shook her shoulder, then she shrugged me off.

I persisted. "Tash!" I whispered forcefully, trying not to let the shivering show in my voice.

"Urgh. Scarlett. What time is it?" Her eyes were still closed as she pulled the duvet over her head.

"You can go back to sleep in a minute, I swear. But I need to know something. What did you find in my room earlier? There *was* something, wasn't there? What did you do with it?" I was speaking too fast. I took a breath and told myself to slow down.

Natasha pulled the duvet back down from her face to look at me. My wide green eyes were staring back at her in the dark.

She hoisted herself up onto her elbows. "You said there was something in your room making you feel odd. You asked me to look, so I looked. Okay?" She yawned.

"What did you find? I know you threw something outside. What was it?" I was talking fast again.

She sighed and sat up, seemingly fully awake now. "I don't know if it was actually the culprit or anything, but I found this black quartz stone thing. My mum is a bit of a hippy and talks about crystals having good and bad energy and all that, so I figured maybe that was what was making you feel weird."

I tried not to give away how happy I was, so I continued to look interested and concerned. "How strange! Oh well, I feel better now, so it must have worked. I wonder why I had it? Maybe it was a present from someone?"

"Okay, I'm glad it wasn't a family heirloom then, because I chucked it on the back of a passing lorry. Can I go back to sleep now?"

This was clearly a courtesy question as Natasha was already turning over and dragging the duvet up to her neck.

"Sure thing. Thanks. And sorry about waking you." I got up slowly, tip-toeing out of her room and back into my, now slightly colder, bed to reflect on this new information. A crystal. A black quartz crystal. *If* Natasha was correct. And someone had broken into our flat to put it there.

The next night in the pub we sat around chatting about films on at the cinema. We had meant to catch the latest Bond installment, but thanks to the long awaited and unexpectedly heavy snowfall throughout the day, we had all arrived too late. So, we convened at our favourite pub, The George, as usual. Natasha and I sat on one side of the table, James and Rafael on the other. We felt festive with our round of mulled wines.

"We've missed out on a drawn-out chase scene, a sex scene, and a big reveal scene," Natasha said. "There you go. I just saved you £14."

"You're not watching properly if you think that's all a Bond film is!" Rafael was flummoxed at her lack of appreciation for Fleming's onscreen protagonist.

"They're not all amazing; you have to admit," James interjected before changing the subject. "How are you guys feeling after the break-in, anyway?"

Natasha's eyes shot over to me. She looked surprised.

"Okay, yeah, I guess," I said. "Bit weird still, especially as the police don't seem to have any idea who it was." I looked at Natasha and mouthed the word *what?* silently.

"But you're doing okay?" James asked.

Natasha broke in. "We're fine, thanks. Locks changed. All good."

I could feel her wanting to change the subject.

She looked around the table. "Are we getting food? I was planning on popcorn for dinner, but if that's not happening, it's Curry Club tonight, and I'm keen for some poppadoms." She reached over for the menu that was wedged between the condiments in the middle of the table.

The sudden mention of curry made me go from not feeling particularly hungry to feeling famished. I looked over her shoulder at what was on offer.

We ordered and chatted about the snow. London had descended into chaos as usual. Trains cancelled, planes delayed. It was as if the city had never seen a snowflake before.

"Oh, I didn't mention yet! I have a date tomorrow!" I said as the food arrived. "Some guy from that dating app. Seems nice enough. He asked me out pretty quickly, but he said it's because of the Christmas break coming up. We'll all be away for a while so he suggested just going for it!"

"Oh, congratulations! I can't wait to hear what's wrong with him." Rafael grinned. "My money is on forgetting his wallet. Oh! Or talking about his ex-girlfriend too much."

I threw my curry-stained napkin at him, which he dodged proficiently.

"You never know. This could be the one?" James was being uncharacteristically optimistic, but I decided to jump on board with him.

"Exactly. This could be the future Mr Gardner."

"You mean you could be the future Mrs Forgot-my-Wallet?"

"No, Rafa. *He* can take *my* name if he wants it, but I'm not taking his. I like being a Gardner, and I will always be a Gardner."

"Alright. Alright." Natasha smiled and patted my head in a jokingly patronising way. We'd had this conversation before.

By the end of the night, we were all overly-stuffed and decided to quit before being tempted by dessert. After saying our goodbyes, Natasha and I made our way down Portobello Road enjoying the newly fallen snow. We chatted about what I would wear on my date. We concluded that he looked fairly casual from his photos, so I shouldn't go all out either, which suited me fine. We were meeting at Gordon's Wine Bar near Charing Cross. It was a great underground cellar-like place to go in winter if it wasn't packed. Upon arriving home and inspecting my wardrobe we decided on a nice black and white polka dot tea dress with tights, dressed down with a denim jacket and Converse. It was a great outfit and implied I was terribly fashionable without even trying. After hanging it all neatly on the back of my bedroom door I climbed into bed and clicked off the bedside lamp.

Sitting in the dimly lit surroundings of the wine bar, I rubbed my aching shoulder. I had managed to fit in a kickboxing session that afternoon and was feeling sore. I looked at all the other couples and wondered what number date they were on. Would they look at us and know it was a first date? Hopefully not. I was early and sat on my own with a glass of wine, looking around in the candlelight, keeping a keen eye on the steps down from the front door. I didn't get too nervous about dating anymore. After so many of them, they'd become routine. I'd lost the politeness factor, opting instead for a simple *'I don't think we're right for each other'* text afterwards as opposed to continuing to chat for weeks with no intention of meeting up again.

I looked down at my phone to check the news sites. Maybe there'd be some good conversation material there, but it was all pretty doom and gloom. Just when I was looking for a good 'skateboarding dog' story, I got a tap on my shoulder.

"Are you Scarlett?"

I turned to see the most handsome man in the bar. He was talking to me. He was smiling, too, giving his face a warm glow. His tan somehow looked natural despite it being mid-December. He had short hair the colour of dark chocolate. His pictures had not done him justice.

I instantly felt uncommonly nervous. "Hi! Yes!" I was too excited. Attempting to calm myself down, I stood up casually and gave him a kiss on the cheek hello. "I mean, hey. Yeah, that's me. You must be Al?"

"I am! You sit back down. The bar doesn't look too busy. Can I get you a drink? I thought maybe we could share a bottle of wine."

"A bottle of white sounds great. You pick which one. I'm not choosey." I immediately regretted that comment.

Al smiled a perfect smile while he hung his brown Barbour jacket on the back of his chair. Then, he headed towards the barman.

I snatched my phone out of my bag.

OMG He's STUNNING! — Me

Haha, definitely something wrong with him then! — Rafa

Wait, stunning like who? — Tash

Zac Efron!?! — Me

Isn't he a child?? — James

No m8, he's all man. Coming back, debrief l8r — Me

Good luck! — Rafa

My date returned with a bucket of ice, two glasses and a bottle of Pinot Grigio.

I jumped straight in with a question to make it look like conversation was already flowing effortlessly.

"Thanks! So, I have to ask, what's 'Al' short for? That's all it had on your profile." I took the bucket from him and placed it between us on the table as he poured wine into both glasses and nestled the bottle into the ice.

"Aleister, spelled funny, though. I prefer Al." He smiled that marvellous smile again—the best I've ever seen. I had to wrench back my composure to carry on the conversation.

"Oh, right!" I wished I had a follow-up question. I hadn't thought this far ahead. I just kept looking at him, wondering if he'd woken up like that or if he'd put an equal amount of preparation into getting ready before our date as I had.

I could feel myself starting to panic. The music in the bar suddenly seemed loud and I realised I couldn't hear myself think let alone come up with sparkling first date conversation. The volume of music increased from loud to deafening. I couldn't hear a word Al was saying, but I smiled politely and nodded my head at him.

He leant over and put his hand on my knee making my stomach flip. "The music is a bit loud in here!" He shouted. "I'm going to ask the barman to turn it down. I want to get to know you!" He got up and disappeared around the corner.

I thought about how much I wanted to get to know him, too. He seemed like a genuinely nice guy, and while he was gone, I managed to calm myself a bit. Deep breaths always helped. I specifically didn't look at my phone, thinking instead about how everyone else in the bar was managing to keep it together. If they could, I could, too. By the time Al came back, the music had returned to its normal background level.

"He said he hadn't touched it! But I guess it's fine now. Anyway, what was I saying?" Luckily, Al seemed completely calm, and, after taking a sip of wine, he continued talking. "Oh right! Scarlett is a lovely name, although with those eyes, I'd have expected your parents to call you 'Esmeralda' or something!"

"Ha, yeah, well, my mum was nuts for *Gone with the Wind* when she was pregnant with me, and Scarlett O'Hara has green eyes, too. That kind of cinched it for her after I was born and she saw me." I had rehearsed this answer in the past, but this time I didn't have the usual bored undertones that conversations with relatives usually harboured. Instead, I smiled and swirled my wine around the glass and tried to pretend it was the first time I'd ever told that story. I became slightly distracted when Al ran his fingers through his hair while I was talking, but then something caught my eye.

"Is that a tattoo?" I gasped, reaching out to hold his wrist for a closer look.

He tugged it away from me. "It's nothing. Silly mistake in Ibiza when I was eighteen. You know what it's like after you finish your A-Levels."

He seemed embarrassed, but I wanted to show him I didn't care. "It's nothing to be ashamed about!" I was full of Dutch courage now. Reaching again to pull up his sleeve, I got a good look at the tattoo on his left wrist of a spider web. "Ooh, spooky! Did a whole bunch of you get the same thing? Don't tell me it was at three in the morning after a night out?"

"Ha. Umm. Something like that. Anyway, can I pour you another drink?"

We went on to talk about where we worked, went to university and grew up. I was telling him all about life in the west country when the bartender came over. He told us politely that it was closing time and asked us to please finish up our drinks. Surprised, I looked at my watch and realised we had rattled through my entire life story and downed another whole bottle of wine. It was probably time to head home before I told him my GCSE results and who my favourite band was.

Outside in the street, the Christmas decorations, coupled with the bottles of wine, made me feel warm and happy despite my choice of fashion over function in the cold weather. The snow had stopped falling a while ago, but the remaining piles dotted about the street gave the scene an elegant serenity often interrupted by London revellers. We had the obligatory "How are you getting home?" conversation and realised we'd be going separate ways. I leant in to give him a kiss on the cheek, putting my hands on his shoulders and smiling goodbye before turning to head down to Embankment Station. There were carollers by the entrance taking donations for charity, so I hummed along. Rummaging about my jacket pocket for change, I dropped some coins in the bucket while cheerily nodding at the singers.

I stood waiting on the platform for the Circle Line train and thought about what a success the evening had been. Compared to the comedy dates I had been on recently, this was more than a success; it was a bona fide delightful date. As I lay in bed that night, clinging to my hot water bottle for warmth and reading the same line in my book over and over again, I relived the evening. I was reconstructing both our conversation and his face in my mind when the bedside table lamp started to brighten. I squinted and tried to ignore it, but the bulb got so bright that it burnt out with a sudden *tzingt!* I continued to lie there, now with my eyes closed, grinning until I fell asleep.

The next morning, I woke up to a brisk chill in the air. Opening the curtains by my bed, I looked out at the street below. More snow had fallen overnight, and the scene looked like a Dickensian portrait of London at Christmas. I would be going home tomorrow to see my parents and Amber, to exchange presents and have a big roast turkey lunch. I was looking forward to it. I was just thinking about how Mum might be planning to jazz it up this year. Last year she boiled the ham in Coke.

I picked up my phone out of habit. Checking WhatsApp, there was some general chatter about when people were free to meet. Amber had sent me a message with a link to an article about all the different ways to eat melted cheese, and Twitter had its usual list of satirical commentaries on serious news topics. I also had a text message. From Al. I didn't expect that. Instantly, I felt my heart race, and I suppressed the urge to giggle. Wanting to savour the feeling, I held off opening it for a moment. It was my experience that guys didn't usually message this soon after a date, even though it was a ridiculous practice. If he *was* interested in me, then why wait the irritatingly customary three days before getting in touch again? If he *wasn't* interested, then good luck ever hearing from him again. I sat up and took a sip of water from the glass next to my bed, pulling the duvet up with me. Once I felt had I revelled in the anticipation for long enough, I unlocked my phone, tapped on the text message icon and took a breath.

Hi Scarlett! Did you get home okay? I know you're heading back to Bristol tomorrow but I wondered if you felt like ice-skating in Hyde Park today? We could meet after lunch? Ax

I kicked my legs up and down under the duvet with excitement, beaming at my phone. "I don't believe it!" I said aloud. Not only had he messaged the next day, but he'd asked me out again for that afternoon! I tried to calm myself and remember that I was, of course, a complete catch, and he would be lucky to get a second date with me. But I couldn't help myself. I was elated that someone so interesting and charming and extraordinarily attractive was this keen to see me again.

He's already txtd asking 4 a 2nd d8 2day! — Me

You're kidding?? Come into my room and tell me about last night! — Tash

No, I want to hear about it! — Rafa

I'll tell u nxt time! Tash, c u after I shwr — Me

Glad it went well! — James

I reread the message another twenty times before rolling out of bed to get ready. Natasha had fixed the shower radio and I sang along cheerfully as I waited for the water to warm up. I had a full ten days off work for Christmas and was just thinking about how this was going to be the best week ever when I realised I had completely forgotten to respond to Al. I clutched at my towel tightly as I rushed to grab my phone from the bedside table. Foolishly, I had presumed that he would know I wanted to go ice-skating, but it was probably wise to let him know it in writing. I tapped out a casually brief reply that had all the makings of "OMG! Yes, I'd love to" but without the painfully obvious enthusiasm and set the phone down by the sink. It was half-past-ten—plenty of time to get ready, pack for my trip home tomorrow, have lunch, panic about my outfit, and then set off to meet Al.

Getting off the tube at Hyde Park Corner in December is like trying to barge your way to the front of a Beyoncé gig. Everyone and their out-of-town seasonal guests were going to Winter Wonderland. I was repeatedly shoved and elbowed just trying to escape out into the open air. It wasn't much better up there either, as the exit was clearly the unofficial meeting point for every man, woman, and child wanting to ride rickety Bavarian rollercoasters, eat currywurst and win stuffed animals. It was cold, but anticipating an afternoon's activities outside on a frozen lake, I had dressed warmer than last night. Natasha and I had decided on black boots, slate grey skinny jeans, and a long black coat. With my blonde hair tousled and a slick of berry red lipstick, I hoped I pulled off my attempt at "Winter Chic."

My gloved hand clumsily held my phone in case it rang, and my eyes darted about the crowd of colourful hats and scarves. The music from various winter-themed rides drifted over me as did the sound of people screaming as they swooped left and right. A particularly loud set of shrieks rang out when I felt a hand spin me round by the shoulder.

"Hey!" Al smiled warmly at me. "You made it! How are you?"

"Great, thanks! Not a lot's happened since I last saw you, though." I joked, but I was pleased to see him again so soon.

Al flashed his winning smile. We started walking in the direction of the fair. "Let's head over to the ice rink while it's quiet, then. I thought we could get a drink and hang out. They have all these cool wooden chalets set up."

"Sounds good! Although I warn you, I haven't ice-skated in years." This was my attempt at laying the groundwork for a serious spectacle of stacking it on the ice. To my surprise and utter, unfettered delight, Al took my hand in his and squeezed it tight.

"I'll make sure you don't fall over."

After twenty minutes of perilous balancing on ice skates and dodging show-offs, the shrill bell rang, and we carefully pushed ourselves over to the exit. We were still laughing at our mock commentary of each other's performances as if we were Olympic skaters; it had kept us totally entertained. A freshly-churned hot chocolate soon turned into a couple of steins of beer and some chips as we poked fun at people's obsession with German Christmas markets. Eventually, it got to the point where I was feeling tipsy. If I was to end the date with dignity, I knew I should probably call it a night.

"I'll walk you over to the station entrance, I'm getting the bus from over the road." Al downed the last few drops of his beer and wiped his mouth with a napkin as he got up to accompany me to the tube.

I ran my fingers through my hair to tame what was probably by now a frizzy nest of blonde curls and re-wrapped my scarf around my neck.

"Thanks. I'm already packed but I need to head off early tomorrow to see the folks for Christmas. My sister already got back from university a few days ago and she'll be going mad on her own there without me."

"Sounds like you'll have a nice time at home. Are you there for New Year's, too?" Al stopped as we got to the Victoria Line entrance and turned to face me.

"Yep, I'll be back on the second." I tried to sound composed. A few flakes of snow began to drift over us again. It had been lightly snowing on and off all afternoon. "I felt like I should put in a decent amount of face time with the family. We'll have some aunts and uncles over and just do something small for New Year's Eve at home."

"That's a shame," said Al, as he let go of my hand and gently placed both of his hands on either side of my face, snowflakes starting to fall heavier around us. "I'll have to take my chance and do this now instead of at midnight then." He leant down and kissed me softly. It was warm and secure, his thumbs stroked my cheeks, and I felt my hands go up to the lapel of his coat to pull him closer and kiss him back. He stopped to lean back and look at me with his deep brown eyes. "Get home safe, and stay in touch while you're away, okay?" His instruction was charming.

I bit my lip and grinned back at him. "Okay." I agreed, letting go of his coat and turning to head down the stairs to the train platforms. It's hard not to look back while walking away from a moment like that but, as I scrunched up my face in celebration, I made absolutely sure not to turn around.

CHAPTER
4

P ADDINGTON TRAIN STATION was bustling with travellers as the
Christmas rush home began. I stood gazing up at the black and
yellow departure board festively decorated with tinsel as I waited for my
train's platform to be announced, my small suitcase nestled between my
ankles and a magazine poking out from my handbag. The twenty-third of
December had collided with a Friday this year, meaning that most travel
arrangements were scheduled for this afternoon, early departure from the
office permitting. Looking around, I saw over-stuffed backpacks, stylish
leather cases, and paper carrier bags brimming with presents, all hurriedly
taken aboard various trains. At that moment, all the numbers and letters
on the board flipped frantically as another service rolled out, and we were
all moved up a spot. A platform was unveiled for my 15:25 to Bristol, so
I clicked up my suitcase handle and began to wheel over to number seven.

Sitting in my seat by the window, I thought about the ten days I was
going to spend at home. Pushing the worries about the break-in from my
head, I thought about how I was going to fill those days and what I wanted
to achieve before coming back to London. I knew I wanted to practice
moving things like I had with the tennis ball and the drawer in my room,
but I felt like this wasn't enough. Since my twenty-first birthday back in
the summer, I'd been feeling like this sort of thing was becoming more
normal. I should be spending more time practicing, but I hadn't been
entirely sure what I was supposed to be practicing. I knew these days at
home in the countryside—in the fresh air and surrounded by nature—

would give me the right environment to make some important progress. And catch up with my family, of course.

Amber was messaging me already to make sure I had caught the train. I sent her a picture of myself with the snowy scenery whizzing past the window behind me as proof that I was on my way. I checked to see if there were any other new messages, but there was nothing. I clicked my phone screen off, put it back in my pocket, and peered out the window at the blanket of white. As hard as I tried, thoughts of who might want to hurt me plagued my journey. Had I hurt them without realising it? Did I have something they wanted? Would they come back? I remembered the newly-installed security cameras and felt reassured that if a prowler came back again, at least we'd be able to catch them.

On arriving back in Bristol, I decided to let the family have a relaxing afternoon and catch a taxi home. Creeping in and surprising them would be fun. As I walked through the front door, I was welcomed by a rush of cooking smells.

"Hello?" I bellowed down the hall as I turned to prop my bag against the stairs and hang up my coat. I heard clattering coming from the kitchen, and the television was on in the living room. I wandered down towards the origin of the homely aroma. Popping my head round the door, I said, "I don't believe you all heard me when I shouted hello just now!"

"Darling! You're home! I was expecting a call to come pick you up!" My mum hastily wiped her hands on her apron as she shuffled over in her slippers to give me a hug.

"It's okay. I just got a cab. You picked me up last time." I turned from one hug immediately into another with Dad. "How's the Christmas rush, Dad? Everyone getting their cards in time?"

"Still one more day to go! Every year I think there's more cards to deliver, you know. Luckily for us the 'Christmas Email' doesn't seem to have caught on." He winked and went back to his job of setting the table for dinner.

I saw Amber had come in from the living room. Her hair was tied up, and she had brightly coloured leggings on.

"Hey, Scar. How's it going?" She looked sporty and was probably going out for a pre-dinner run.

It was good to see her again. I pulled her in for the biggest hug of all and a theatrical kiss on the cheek. "Bamber! Great now you're here!" I said only semi-sarcastically.

She smiled as she always did when I used her childhood nickname. It came from when I had a horrible cold and could only pronounce her name with a "B" at the start. It had, since then, morphed into all sorts of variations: Bams, Bambi, Bamborella. She never minded any of them because she knew how much I loved her. "How's uni? Are you enjoying Loughborough? I can see from Facebook you're having fun!" I poked her teasingly in the ribs as she laughed nervously. I had seen photos of her in some pretty scandalous fancy dress online. I winked at her, clapping my hands together. "So, what's for dinner?"

Mum's family dinners were a thing to behold. Timing alone was an impressive skill. She had every meat, side and sauce ready at the same time. The imagination she had for dishes was also a constant source of wonder. She would tell me that it all came down to what was in the fridge and a little creativity. Me, I would just eat things separately: sausages, eggs, broccoli. But Mum would weave things together into a tapestry of flavours. They all fell under the umbrella term, "casseroles."

"This is nice, Mum," I said through a mouthful. "What's in it?"

"Well, I had some leftover risotto so I made arancini balls. They have cheese in the middle."

I took another delicious bite and breadcrumbs scattered across my plate. "See? I'd have settled for warmed up risotto. Or, more likely, cold risotto. You are good at this kitchen stuff." I teased her.

"It's called cooking, dear. You might have to learn about it sometime." She smiled and turned the conversation towards Amber and her first term of university. I remember hearing about the traumatic ordeal of leaving her there on the first day of Fresher's Week. Mum cried. Dad worried about the parking meter. Amber was desperate for everyone to leave so she could get on with meeting her new flatmates. Not too different from when I was dropped off at Leeds for my first term. I knew she'd settle in quickly, though. With all the netball and hockey she loves doing, she'd make friends in no time.

After dinner, we congregated in the living room to watch Friday night television. I sat, knees pressed up against my chest, in the corner of the sofa reading my book as my parents settled down to the satirical round-up of the week's news. Amber was texting someone she thought was cute. I could tell by the way she was smiling at her phone and checking it every three minutes. I knew that Dad would clock this soon enough and tease her endlessly about it.

I looked around the cosy room—the faded blue carpet that I did forward rolls on as a kid, the dark red, striped sofa that I spilled a whole cup of blackcurrant squash on once and was relieved the colours matched so Mum would never know. The Christmas tree was stood in the bay window decorated in silver and gold, a pile of presents already wrapped and lying underneath the gently twinkling fairy lights. I had been thoughtful yet economical with my gifts this year due to my considerable lack of pennies. Mum had got a nice top from Coast that had been on sale a while ago. Dad got a fancy pair of padded insoles for his work boots, although I knew he'd joke about how he'd only need one. Finally, Amber was the lucky recipient of a book of drinking games to play at Loughborough. I knew these weren't the best presents they could have hoped for, but they understood that I had not started earning a lot just yet. They would still open them with beaming faces and thank me as if I'd given them each a bar of gold.

That night, as I lay in my old bedroom staring at the cloud design I had painted on the ceiling in blue and white when I was thirteen, I was excited about the coming few days. What could I achieve now that I had more time and fewer distractions? I also thought about the crystal that had been put in my room, reminding myself that something, or rather someone, was interfering with me, and they were doing it in a menacing way to scare me. I knew I had to work on my "abilities," but, when I thought about the break-in, I knew that I had to work fast. This was not a situation where I could rely on someone else to protect me. I had to do it myself.

Christmas Eve has always had a certain magic about it. People have a bounce in their step. They hold doors open for others, and they say hello cheerily to passers-by in the street. Mum, Dad and Amber had gone to do some last-minute shopping at the supermarket for the big lunch tomorrow afternoon, and I had the house to myself. That feeling of "seasonal energy" fuelled me as I sat in my bedroom trying to clear my mind and centre myself. I sat very still at my old desk, surrounded by shelves of used textbooks and framed photographs. I focused on my breath, and on the molecules of air rushing into my lungs and then back out into the room. I thought about the blood pulsing through me, of the cells travelling along veins and around my body, oxygenating my muscles and my brain. I opened my eyes and looked at the mug of tea on my desk brought to me by my lovely mum this morning but forgotten about until now, leaving it cold and wasted. The surface was reflective and motionless, and I thought about what makes up tea. The water molecules of hydrogen and oxygen, infused with dried tea leaves and milk, sat drifting idly in the mug. I thought about the energy I felt in myself, the life I had coursing through me, and I targeted those resting molecules of water. I imagined the transfer of power, of intensity and activity, to breathe life into these molecules and make them move.

For about three minutes I sat there.

Nothing.

Had I failed?

I continued to focus.

The faintest plume of steam began rising from the mug.

I smiled and reached out to tentatively touch the side of the mug. It wasn't scalding, but it was hot. I knew I'd done it. I was so proud of myself that I shuffled happily about in my seat and took a victory sip of hot tea. At that moment, I heard a key turning in the front door and people rustling in with shopping bags.

"We're home!" Mum sang up the stairs.

"Ok! Be right down!" I stood up and let my blonde hair down, brushing it crudely with my fingers. I felt accomplished and happy. Things were clicking. It all felt so natural. My next task would be to practice levitation again, only this time faster, so that I could do it on command and without five minutes' preparation time. I spent the rest of the day practising, either in my room, out on a walk, down the garden, even just lying in bed. I improved. A lot. It was dawning on me that, with practice, almost anything could be possible.

Christmas morning began with the usual smell of bacon wafting up the stairs and the sound of BBC Radio 2 bouncing off the walls of the kitchen. Pulling the warm duvet up around my neck, I blinked my eyes open and shut them again to try to go back to sleep. It only took a few seconds to register the music and remember what day it was. The little kid in me instantly woke up. I pushed the covers off, swung my legs round off the bed and into my slippers, and yawned my way downstairs. Entering the kitchen, I saw Mum transferring the bacon from the frying pan to the paper towel while trying to avoid Dad's pinching fingers when the toast popped up.

"I see I'm right on time," I said, making them jump slightly.

"Merry Christmas, Scarlett! Come here and give me a hug." Mum wiped her hands on the tea towel hanging next to the stove and I went over to give her little frame a squeeze. I turned to Dad and did the same, although he was much bigger than Mum and still liked to pick me up.

"Happy Christmas, Dad." I wheezed as I was mid-air. He lowered me back to my feet gently with a laugh. "Is Amber up yet?"

"Haven't seen her, but we did hear some movement earlier so she might be up." Dad turned back to pinching whatever was coming out of the frying pan while I pulled out a plate to construct a traditional Christmas morning bacon butty.

As I sat at the kitchen table, the front door rattled opened, and then banged shut. We all looked, puzzled, towards the kitchen door as Amber came through breathing heavily. Her cheeks were flushed a rosy pink. She was dressed in black leggings with a neon yellow body warmer. I could hear the tinny sound of dance music pulsing from her headphones. She didn't use Christmas as an excuse to ditch her early morning run.

"Merry Christmas!" I greeted her with a mouthful of buttery bread and bacon. I smiled at the contrast between sisters. I liked to workout but certainly had my lazy moments. Amber just had this font of energy that built up inside her, and she was constantly having to work it off.

"Happy Christmas, Scar." She came over to give me a hug and a kiss.

Her frozen cheek pressed up against mine made me recoil with a squeal. "You're like ice!"

"Well, it's bloody cold out there, isn't it?"

"Amber!" Mum gave her 'the look.' She didn't like even the mildest of swearing.

"Sorry!" Amber took her gloves and shoes off and left them by the back door before heading upstairs to shower.

I loved this scene. Everyone at home, bustling about independently but perfectly mingling together. We all had our jobs, which is what happens after a while. Those designated "good at cooking"—Mum and

Amber—prepared the feast. The rest of us set the table, walked the dog, and generally tidied up. After Amber reappeared to eat something for breakfast, we all gathered in the living room to open presents. It wasn't quite the epitome of excitement it once was for us as children. Gone were the two frantic little girls dying to get in to see the presents under the tree after Santa brought them during the night. We now sat politely and opened gifts in turns, explaining the thought behind each gift and thanking the giver. But presents weren't what Christmas was about for us as a family anymore. The point was being together, having our silly traditions and, for a few days, not thinking about work or other dramas happening in our daily lives. This was a time for us to be just "The Gardners."

The rest of the day passed at a pleasingly ambulatory pace. We messed around with our new gifts: either trying on clothes, reading the first few pages of books or setting up new electronics. Mum migrated back to the kitchen to continue the Great Preparations along with Amber who oversaw sauces, jellies and spreads. Despite my constant reminders that these all came pre-made, she insisted on beginning from scratch. And they always did taste better.

It was my job to do some tidying up, so when I was alone in the living room, after double checking no one else was around, I had a couple of tries with the discarded wrapping paper and gift tags on the floor. I thought about how to pick it all up without touching it. I imagined lifting from below, moving the air molecules and creating an upwards force to float all the discarded detritus into the air. I had only intended to do one item at a time, but every piece of paper started to hover. Having only ever moved one thing at a time, I felt proud that I could manage this number of things at once. So, feeling bold, I carried on lifting them higher. Soon, every ripped piece of wrapping paper, name tag and other piece of discarded Christmas debris was two meters high. Static at first, they started swirling around the centre of the room. I stood staring, amazed that I was conducting this whirlpool of multi-coloured litter above my head. It was beautiful.

"Scarlett!" Dad called my name.

I heard the familiar *thud-thump* of his footsteps nearing the living room. My eyes snapped towards the door and the colourful debris froze momentarily in the air before raining down to the floor.

The door opened.

"Scarlett, can you come give me a hand with . . . What on earth are you doing in here? I thought you were tidying up, not making it worse!" Dad scratched his head and looked about the room, which looked much messier than before.

"Oh, yeah. I haven't started yet, sorry. Um, I was on my phone." I held my head down, looking around my feet.

"Okay, well just carry on then. When you're done, I need help with this pedometer thing your mother got me."

"Of course, Dad. I'll be right there." I was already bending over to scoop up the pieces of rubbish, stuffing it all into a recycling bag.

"Oh, and Scarlett?" He turned, one hand resting against the door frame, his eyes smiling at me.

"Yes, Dad?"

"You've got wrapping paper on your head." He left laughing. I reached up with my fingers and felt the scrap of paper with tape clinging to my hair.

That had been close. I made a note to myself not to get carried away again, otherwise, I'd have some explaining to do. I wasn't quite ready for that.

Lunch was a blur of food, hats and bad jokes. Jet sat patiently next to my Dad's side hoping he would pass down some turkey out of pity, or at least drop some out of clumsiness. Mum and Amber had outdone themselves once again, making both a turkey and a ham, with pigs in blankets, stuffing, potatoes, carrot and Swede mash, plus the usual bucket of gravy. I thought about the number of hours in the gym it would take to sweat all this off, but that was swiftly booted from my mind in the name of a one-off good old Christmas lunch. It was a holiday and a festive time for over indulging. That's why I loved this time of year. Dessert always had to come a few hours later when we could face it. Usually, a chocolate log or brandy pudding. Dinner was "scraps in sandwiches" around eight o'clock when inexplicable hunger began to creep in again. We would, for the next few days, continue to eat the same lunch in various forms. My mum made all manner of curries, casseroles and salads with leftover Christmas lunches. One year, I was given turkey curry in March because we'd had so much left over, it had gone in the freezer.

After an evening watching classic Christmas movies on TV—*Home*

Alone was always my favourite—we finished off our favourite *Quality Streets* and went to bed. I put my phone on the bedside table and noticed the message light blinking. My phone had been buzzing most of the day with Natasha and Rafael discussing their differing ways of celebrating, however, this was a text. A text from Al. I sat down on the bed and tapped it open.

> *Happy Christmas! Hope you're having a great day with the fam. Looking forward to seeing you when you get back. A x*

Perfect, I thought as my eyes danced back along the message. It was appropriately brief but friendly with the bonus of mentioning another date on the cards.

> *Sure* 😊 *— I'll let u no wen I'm bck in Ldn. Hope ur having a gd xmas 2! Scar x*

Plugging in my phone to charge on the bedside table, I brushed my teeth, got into bed with a book and read contentedly until I fell asleep, the paperback slowly slipping out of my hands.

The following days were spent in holiday limbo. Christmas was over, but New Year's Eve was still a few days away. I had five days to dedicate my time to practising my new-found skills. My parents were busy either with work or organising family members for New Year's, so I was free to spend my time in peaceful solitude or catching up with Amber. I even managed to forget about the break-in completely, meaning I finally felt completely relaxed.

One day when I was at a loose end and Amber had been studying all morning in her room, I slinked in and slumped onto her bed. "Whatcha doin'?" I whined at her. She turned around smiling, dropping her pencil into the middle of her open textbook, signifying a pause in studies.

"Working. I have a couple of assignments to do over the holiday. Nothing too hard, but they take time. How are you? Bored, by any chance?"

"No, not bored! I want to know what's new with my little sister? I know you're into someone. You keep smirking while you text. C'mon, tell me, who is it?" I sat up to better read her face when she replied. Amber was smart, but she struggled to hide what she was really thinking. True to form, her mouth broke into a reluctant smile. I knew I'd wormed my way through her protective wall.

"Argh. Yes. Okay. There's someone I like, but it's really new, and I'm not talking about it yet." She turned to face her books again.

"Come on, tell me about him. What's his name? What's he studying?" I pleaded with her.

Amber looked down at her notes and tapped her pencil on the paper thoughtfully. "I'm not ready yet," she replied calmly but insistently.

I got the sister-sense that I should back off. I rose cheerfully to my feet, clapping my hands together. "Okay! Well, lunch is ready if you want to come down. I'm promised there is at least one 'non-leftover' component to it today, but that may just be the bread."

"I'll be down in a minute."

I left her room closing the door behind me and hoped I hadn't upset her somehow. Amber had always been cagey about her love life. I trusted that one day she would be open with me, but I respected that it would take time.

Later that day, I took Jet for a walk in the fields around our house, letting him off the lead for a good run about. I sat on the usual bench for a rest at the top of the hill, contemplating what else I could do while I was home. I loved sitting there. I could hear the melody of nature playing, the sound of animals rustling and dogs barking. If I concentrated, I could hear the grass growing and the worms turning the earth. Not just hear it—I could feel it. I tried to attune myself to Nature's harmonious symphony, to be one with my surroundings. Soon, my breath was yet another instrument in the aria I could hear. An overwhelming feeling that I was truly in control of life washed over me. I *knew* I could protect myself. I had control over my life for certain, but maybe . . . just maybe I was in control of other things, too.

I opened my eyes and saw Jet standing about ten feet away from me, wagging his tail, his tongue hanging out his mouth as he panted. I looked at his handsome face and those big doe-eyes.

He turned to look straight back at me.

I maintained eye contact with him for a few seconds. Then, I had an idea. "SIT," I thought.

He closed his mouth and sat down.

I continued to look him in the eyes.

He wagged his tail and seemed to await another instruction.

"LIE DOWN," I thought.

Jet shuffled his front paws further away until he slid onto his belly.

I could feel him acquiesce. He was a pack animal following orders, and those orders didn't have to be verbal. I looked at his adorable, loving face, the face I'd spent my teens growing up with, and I smiled at him. "HOME TIME," I thought, a bit louder this time.

Jet came bounding over to me. He rubbed his neck against my leg until I reattached the leash. He was excited to get his post-walk treat when we got home.

"Good boy, Jet! Let's go home!" I scratched him roughly behind the ears as he started pulling me in the direction of home. I still felt a bit dazed, wrenching myself back to normal by muting the sounds around me. After holding my breath in concentration, fresh air rushed into my lungs, and I perked up enough to have a skip in my step as we made our way back. I thought about how many of us go about our everyday lives having to ignore most of what happens around us so we aren't deafened by the noise of the daily chaos in our brains. What's for dinner? What time do I have to pick up the kids from school? Are all of the bills paid this month? But among the bedlam is the music of the natural world around us, melodies all too often silenced. By tuning out the daily clamour of a busy life, I could truly connect to the part of me that was able to control things better—my thoughts and, it seemed, other things, too. But to function in society with a job and a social life, I had to ignore the roar of nature around me. The din of modern life was blocking it all out. It dawned on me that I should be open to all of it. All the time. I should hear the beep of my phone as well as feel the vibrations in the air. To be in command of it all was surely my aim; this was what I tried to hone in on during the last few days I had at home. I had to use this time wisely.

Our modest New Year's Eve party consisted of me, Mum, Dad and Amber, plus some aunts and uncles, and a few neighbours. The cocktail sausages and crisps were out on the dining room table, and the music was blaring throughout the house. People started arriving around nine o'clock. I heard them bustle through the door as I finished getting ready. Mum would be pleased I'd bought a special dress for the evening. Plus, I was wearing the teal coloured earrings she had given me as a Christmas present, so this should put her in a pretty good mood. I spritzed on some perfume. As I was re-pinning my hair, I heard my name bellowed up the stairs. I was running behind and knew I should already be downstairs to help greet people and take their coats. This had always been my job. After my coat-check duties, I switched to roving waitress, handing out canapés and serving drinks. Having these jobs gave me an excellent reason to dodge all awkward conversations about my personal life.

"Scarlett! Everyone's arrived at once! I need your help, PLEASE come downstairs!" Mum sounded distressed. Amber was obviously not being entirely useful and was probably playing her usual trick of finding somewhere to hide (like the pantry). She would profess that she was only looking for more toast points when really she was sat playing with her phone until someone found her out. I imagined our downstairs hallway right now. People muddling around each other over-enthusiastically greeting those they hadn't seen in ages. It all sounded very loud and overwhelming. The thought struck me, "What if I could go downstairs without anyone seeing me? Was it possible?"

I stood at my bedroom door with one hand on the door handle, ready to open it and enter the mayhem going on in the rest of the house. Closing my eyes, I conjured up a shield—a sort of reflective sphere that went all the way around me. I imagined that I was trapped in one of those washing-up bubbles, only it was six-feet high. I thought about it surrounding me, gleaming in an opaque, pearlescent-white colour. It was echoing images all around me. When I was quite sure it was stable, I held it in my mind and turned the handle to go downstairs.

Everything looked slightly different. I was reminded of the rainbow of colours I'd seen in oil stains in the light. Edges blurred into one another. The blue of the carpet bled into the white of the walls, but I could still see everything happening around me.

I walked down the stairs, the noise of merry visitors echoing faintly within my bubble.

Treading carefully between relatives, I made sure not to bump into anyone.

I heard my mum in the distance complaining about how I wasn't helping her, so I drifted to the kitchen. She was standing by the oven checking the timer.

My Aunty Sue passed me as she left the kitchen.

Not a single person had spoken with me or even looked me in the eye by this point, and I realised that I had created a delusory mirror around myself.

Enough. It was time to break the bubble, which meant breaking my concentration. I shook my head with my eyes shut tight and cleared my throat, grateful to be able to relax again.

"Ahem!" I coughed to wake up my throat and send a little shock through my body, but nothing happened. Everyone continued to move around me, oblivious as I tried to get their attention.

I closed my eyes and focused all my energy on bursting the bubble, but I could still feel it around me. I imagined a stream of light running from my heart to the sphere, like an umbilical cord fuelling the shield. I visualised myself with a large pair of gleaming silver scissors, hovered the cord of light between the two sharp metallic blades and forcefully slammed the two handles down.

The connection was severed, restoring the room around me to its usual defined edges and clear colours.

Mum fumbled the timer and sent it flying into the air as she clung to the side of the oven. "Good God, Scarlett! You frightened the life out of me! How long have you been standing there? For heaven's sake, go and help people with their coats. They're leaving them all over the place." She held her hand to her chest and exhaled deeply, her raised eyebrows creasing her forehead.

I felt badly for scaring her, but I was relieved to have reappeared. Smiling apologetically, I immediately went to join the ruckus of guests and mingle like I was supposed to. After all, it was very nice to see everyone before I left for London the next day. I just had to manage a few hours dodging awkward questions first.

Midnight eventually came and went, just as it did every evening, except this time we all cheered merrily, hugged, held hands and began the New Year singing and laughing. My parents were happy and smiling. Mum looked over from across the room and mouthed "Happy New Year" to me.

I smiled back and blew her a kiss. I was glad she could see me.

CHAPTER
5

B ACK IN LONDON, the January blues were settling in. Long gone was the merriment of Christmas. No more did bartenders cheerfully greet me as I walked into my favourite pub, nor did colleagues at the museum ask excitedly about my holiday plans. Strangers no longer greeted each other on the street with wishes of good will. Instead, the city felt filled with people who were broke, tired and hungover. The falling snow, that only a couple of weeks ago lifted our spirits, now only served to make commutes more difficult. Sad-looking Christmas trees, their needles scattered around them, were discarded on the pavement along with all the usual rubbish.

I walked to the tube station on the afternoon of the second day in January feeling a noticeable change in the air. The joy was gone. The world's problems, which had been put on hold for the holidays, were back. Strings of fairy lights hanging in neighbouring windows now seemed a meagre attempt to cling to the magic of Christmas, although they had probably been forgotten about. Fellow passengers on the train to work coughed and sniffed, and stared at their copy of the *METRO* newspaper to see what had been going on in the world, slotting right back into their daily rituals. The front page covered a disaster that had happened at a New Year's Eve party abroad somewhere. The full-page photo of a nightclub on fire was harrowing, showing people fleeing for their lives. I thought about my own little New Year's party at home and how lucky I was to have had all our family in the same place to celebrate. I was still squinting at the writing on the page when I saw we were at my stop. I leapt up and shuffled my things out onto the platform.

Work was still busy since most kids weren't back at school yet and tourists who had chosen London as their New Year's holiday destination still had a day or two before returning to their home country. At least on the first day back at work, conversation amongst my colleagues was easy. I told Esther about our lovely big lunch and the comedy leftovers situation. She said her family are originally from Latvia, so they have their own traditions. This was fascinating, although I tried not to laugh when she referred to the "Christmas Old Man" bringing the presents. I frowned sympathetically when she told me about how, as a child, she'd had to sing and dance and recite poems to receive her presents. I thought about how Amber and I launched into our gifts as soon as we were allowed in the living room and suddenly felt a little spoilt.

"Do you have the typical turkey and stuffing for lunch, though?" I asked as we sat at the front desk. There was a lull in visitors as they found their way to various eateries for lunch.

"Oh no, but I wish we did. I used to get that at school before the end of term in December, and it was really good. My mum makes the traditional Latvian lunch. Peas with bacon, some mini pie things, cabbage, sausage, and then gingerbread for after." She was telling me this while scanning through her work emails on the computer, however, she turned to look at me once she had registered my stunned silence.

My wide, green eyes stared at her. "Pies and Cabbage? You poor thing, Esther. No wonder you preferred your school dinners. Although, I am on board with the sausage and gingerbread." I smiled, suddenly worried I'd insulted her home nation's choice of Christmas food.

Esther laughed and continued to search through her inbox.

"What are you looking for?" I asked.

"Didn't you get this email over the holiday? Hell of a time to send it. They said something about cutting our hours down as well as extending opening times. No idea how they'll manage it, but sounds like we're going to be spread pretty thin."

"What? No, I didn't get that! That's such crap. I only make just about enough to afford my rent as it is." I immediately started searching through my unread emails. There it was.

Dear Employees,

Due to unforeseen cut backs here at the West London Art &
Archaeology Museum, it has become necessary to implement
certain changes. As of 1st Feb, those currently on "Casual
Contracts" will have reduced hours. Also, in order to allow the
public more time to visit us, we are extending our opening times
from 8 a m to 9:30 p m. This means shift times are also subject to
change.

We appreciate your cooperation.

Management

I read the email several times to make sure I had understood it
correctly. "Casual Contracts" were how the bosses gutlessly referred to
"Zero Hours Contracts," meaning we were never guaranteed a single
hour of work. If we wanted a decent work schedule, we had to be in the
good graces of Jackie, the manager, who did the rota.

"We appreciate your cooperation? They do like to presume we'll
cooperate, don't they? It's a handy consequence of having no choice in
the matter." I slumped back in my chair.

Esther was printing the email so she could show it to her husband
later. She looked worried, which wasn't surprising.

I was worried, too. "Are you okay on the desk for a while? I'm going
to do a quick 'presentation check.'"

"Sure, you go ahead. It's not busy." Esther rose to lean over towards
the whirring printer.

"Thanks." I stood up and used the excuse for a walk around to clear
my head. What was I going to do? Well, I had a month to figure it out. I'd
hate to leave this place. I loved working here, but management kept
making it so difficult for me to stay on. First, they put me on a casual
contract, so I had no job security. Then, they made me double-up on
duties, alternating between the front desk as well as the stewarding of the
exhibits. It seemed as if every change was for the worse, spreading people
thinner and thinner, all in the name of what? Profit, I'm sure.

I went to knock on the manager's door. "Jackie? Do you have a moment?" I creaked the door open gently to see if she was in.

"Sorry? Oh, yes. Hi, Scarlett. What can I do for you?" She was rustling papers around her unorganised desk.

"It's about the email we got over the holidays. Did you know about it?" I tried to sound hurt, so she didn't realise I was angry.

"Oh. That. No. I didn't. Except, of course, it's now my job to roster people for it. I don't even know if we have enough people to cover that long a day." Jackie rubbed her temples with her fingers and continued to stare down at her desk. I could see she was stressed, and I realised that she shouldn't be the target of my anger. She was a replaceable cog, like rest of us, being given instructions and expected to follow them.

"Is there any chance it'll change? Like, they might change their minds? Or are we definitely going to get fewer hours every week?" I looked at her in the eye, and I could feel her apologising before she even spoke.

"I'm sorry, Scarlett. This is from above my head. I just have to implement it." She paused. Probably sensing a lack of managerial demeanour, she sat up straighter. "Is there anything else I can help you with today?" She sounded more formal, less compassionate.

"No. Thank you." I turned on my heels to leave. Jackie wasn't on my side, but she clearly had her own battles to fight.

For the rest of the day, I took tickets until it was my turn to check around the rooms again. I stopped by the Inca exhibit for longer than the others, as was my routine. My head was still whirring with thoughts about work as I looked at the artefacts, wondering whether I'd manage to pay the rent with fewer hours. I hated asking for money from my parents. Plus, it was unreasonable to ask them to supplement my income indefinitely. No, that was out of the question. I'm not sure they even knew how much I was struggling financially. I exhaled loudly and resolved to just do my best. There wasn't a lot more I could do. I was an adult, and I would have to take care of myself.

At home, Natasha could tell something was up. She fussed around me as if I were sick, even though I told her everything was fine. We had already had our Christmas debrief session, and everything had gone, rather depressingly, back to normal.

Until she brought in a box and dumped it in the corner.

"My mum was going to throw these books away. I know you love reading, so I figured I'd bring them here to see if you wanted any. Don't expect the literary greats, or anything, though. My mum is pretty 'New Age' these days." Natasha opened the box she brought from her trip home for the holidays, and I peered inside.

I had always liked her mum. She seemed caring and generous, and I was interested in what her library consisted of, even if it was out of my comfort zone. "Thanks, Tash. I just finished re-reading *A Christmas Carol*, so maybe I'll go with something a bit different next." I wasn't expecting to find anything I wanted to read in there, but I would look out of courtesy.

After Natasha went to bed, I finished my tea, turned the TV off and tidied the living room up. Just as I was about to switch the light off, I looked down into the box just to glance at a few titles to see what was in there. The top books were self-help manuals. Poor Natasha's mum was going through a divorce, and they seemed to be mainly about regaining control of one's life. I pushed those aside and continued exploring. A few chick lit beach reads. Some Dan Brown novels. And then, a couple of books that caught my eye.

Understand Crystals and their Effect on the Human Energy Shield

The dark green book's cover had the outline of a person standing tall, waves of energy emanating from their body. I thought about Natasha's knowledge about the crystal in my room. She must have learned about it from her mum. Maybe this book would be useful? I picked it up, tucked it under my arm and kept looking. Moving aside some more self-help copies, I saw something even more intriguing.

The Solitary Witch: A Guide for the Novice

I stared wide-eyed at the title and read it a few times. Why would she have this? Was I a solitary witch? Was this what I was doing? I knew about witches from films and stories, but they were always luring children into gingerbread houses or surrounded by flying monkeys. Was I just a wartless, non-green, innocent version of them? I couldn't relate to those characters at all, but something drew me to the book. I continued to stare at the front cover. There was a woman standing barefoot in the grass; she was dressed in a long flowing dress. Trees and bushes surrounded her while the moon's beam bathed her in light. I felt comforted. If someone said to me, "This lovely woman is a witch," then I'd be inclined to think maybe I was one. But I had no idea *why* I was one. It didn't make sense. I pushed the idea of labels out of my mind.

I picked up the book, skim-read the back and squeezed it under my arm along with the one about crystals. My mind began to race, and I took time to breathe to slow it down. There was no rush. I needed to take my time to learn as much as I could. That night, I settled in under my duvet with my hot water bottle and new books. I began reading slowly, making sure to absorb every word.

I woke to the sun already risen late the next morning, excited by what the books had revealed to me. I had learned so much about attuning with nature and worshipping the earth. I had never known anyone who spoke like that. I even read about some rituals that I would make time to try out. Finally, I felt like I had answers. Answers to questions I hadn't realised I'd been asking my whole life.

I sat up in bed and looked at my phone. There was a new message from Al. We had been texting back and forth a bit; it was half-chat and half-trying to find a time we were both free to meet. I already had plans with Rafael and James after work today, so I texted him back to say I could see him over the weekend if he was free. I knew I wanted to spend the rest of the week reading. As I looked over at the two books sat on my nightstand, I laughed. I guess these were *my* self-help manuals.

Downstairs, Natasha was in her pyjamas eating cereal and watching the news. She looked up at me as I came in and smiled. "Morning!" She said looking cheery. "Did you find anything you like in there?" She gestured towards the box of soon-to-be-charity-shopped books.

I hesitated briefly, not wanting to lie, but also not quite ready to admit to which ones I had taken.

"Hey! A couple of titles caught my eye. I might have another look later," I offered as consolation. I wished I could tell her which books I'd taken and why. I wished I could share with my closest friend that I had this enormous secret. But I knew that once I did, I could never take it back.

Natasha turned her attention back to the TV.

"Are you coming to this gig tonight? It's at Scala next to King's Cross." I changed the subject.

"Can't. I have to go meet an old uni mate at nine. She's in town for the night, so we're catching up."

"Ah, nice. Yeah, I thought about going to visit my sister at uni in Loughborough, actually." I winked at Natasha, and she laughed. We'd both discussed our university transgressions in depth and had decided it was probably the most fun we'd ever had. I went to make myself a smoothie for breakfast and head to the gym before work. I needed to clear my head, and it had been a while since I'd punched or kicked anything.

I thought about everything I'd read the night before as I whiled away my shift at work. I was looking forward to getting back to studying. From what I could tell so far, the book was about connecting with nature and with yourself. And although I'm not sure it gave everyone who read it the ability to do the sort of things I could do, it was probably meant for empowerment and strength and generally improving people's lives without the kind of special effects magic seen in the movies. Luckily, it helped me the way it was probably meant to help other readers: through building confidence and focusing attention where it's most needed.

And there was something else. The word *magick*. It was new to me. I soon realised that mysterious *k* differentiated it from regular magic. Card tricks. Sawing people in half. Those were illusions for entertainment, tricking people into thinking they'd seen something they hadn't. That *k* made it special, transformative. It made it *my* kind of magick.

At work, the general mood among my colleagues was still gloomy. Mostly, people were asking around to see if anyone knew of any other jobs going. I felt sad thinking about the break-up of the nice little work group we had. We didn't tend to socialise much outside of the museum, but we all enjoyed each other's company and got on well. It would be a shame not to see them all again, in the same place, helping each other get through the day. I resigned myself to believing this was just life. People come. People go. But it was sad all the same. I thought about what I might do. Should I also try to find another job? Would it be wiser to stick it out here to see if I could survive on the reduced pay? None of it sounded terribly appealing.

I shook the thought from my head and checked my watch. Not long to go until the gig. I had wanted to stop by a shop on the way, too, to pick up some candles. Different colours symbolised different intentions or results, apparently. Orange was for joy and success. Pink was for any form of love. I had to be careful, however, with that sort of thing until I knew what I was doing. I had read that any romance spells tend to backfire because you can't force someone to feel love. Even with magick. I started to wonder about what I could do with actual guidance and tools. Until now, all of my progress had been just me figuring it out as I went along. I got a chill thinking about it.

A few hours later, I was queuing in the freezing cold waiting for the others to turn up. I constantly checked my phone to make sure no one was cancelling last minute. Rubbing my hands together, I blew into them to inject some warmth into my palms, but my breath just left my hands a bit clammy. Eventually, Rafael turned up, followed shortly by James. We stood a few feet from the entrance enjoying the gusts of heat coming from inside. When we got to the front, the security guard stuck a flashlight into my handbag and poked around in it. Then, he asked us all for ID.

Rafael's eyes widened in disbelief. He turned to look at me. "I forgot it!" he exclaimed.

"What do you mean? Where's your driving license?" I thought he must have something in his wallet to prove his age.

"I sent it away to change the address on it. Oh shit, I meant to bring my passport, but I forgot!"

"Can't come in without ID, Sir." The security guard crossed his muscular arms.

"He's clearly over eighteen!" I couldn't believe the pettiness, but I knew from friends who spent the odd summer working the door at clubs back home that once you ask for ID, you have to see it. Can't go back on it after that.

"Come on, please? I'm twenty-two!" Rafael pleaded.

"Can't come in without ID, Sir," he repeated, his voice lowered and a bit sterner.

Rafael looked at me, desperately running his fingers through his hair repeatedly.

Poor Rafael. Clearly, he was distraught. I turned to look back at the six-foot-four man blocking the entry. He was only doing his job, but I really wanted Rafael to come in. I looked him in the eye. "Excuse me, Sir? This man is twenty-two. You can let him in."

"I . . . don't have to," said the bouncer, but he sounded confused, and his eyes were darting back and forth between Rafael and me.

It was working. I looked through his pupils, the feeling of acceptance flowing from me to him. I felt a shift in him, and I kept talking. I could see in the corner of my eye James and Rafael were a few feet away, rummaging through his wallet for anything that proved his age.

"Sir, you know this man is twenty-two. You don't need to see ID. Can we come in?" I didn't blink as I spoke to him.

His eyes, cold and hard to begin with, had softened, and they looked down at me in neutral. "Yes, Miss. On you go. All of you. Next!" I turned to grab the boys and drag them through while we still could.

James turned to me by the cloakroom. "What just happened? I thought Rafa couldn't get in?"

"Yeah, I didn't show him any ID!"

Both stood looking confused, so I told them I used my feminine wiles to charm the doorman. "He just needed a bit of convincing!" I winked at them.

We paid to put our coats in the cloakroom and headed up the stairs to the main room, stopping off on the way to grab a drink. Rafael insisted on paying for mine, as a thank you. It was also to persuade me to never use my charms on him.

"Who knows what you'd have me do! I'd be cleaning your whole flat in no time!" He laughed, knowing full well he'd already been charmed into tasks like this by girls he liked. I reminded him of these times. He went to see *CATS!* even though he hated musicals. He put together a whole bookcase for a girl who broke it off with him soon after. Rafael laughed and shook his head. "Oh yeah . . . I'd just do it anyway. No charm needed!"

"Women and their spells, hey?" James said, looking directly at me.

I suddenly felt nervous. I really shouldn't have done that. I couldn't believe it. In front of who knows how many people! Did James know what I'd done? Could he tell I'd done something other people can't do?

My mind went into overdrive with worry, and I had to make a real effort to enjoy the gig so everything seemed normal. The look in James' eye kept playing in my head. Why had he used the word "spell?" I guess it did fit the conversation, but it was so specific. I didn't even know if I had used a spell, although maybe it counted as one. I had to stop thinking about it. I'm sure the concerned look on my face was going to invite more attention, and I just wanted everyone to focus on the band playing onstage.

We danced and sang along, cheering and clapping after each song. With a couple more drinks in me, I managed to relax a bit. We all had a good time, but I couldn't wait to get home. I made a mental note never to use my will to influence anyone again. Not only was it selfish to manipulate a man who was only doing his job, but it was Rafael's fault he'd forgotten his ID. I felt like kicking myself for acting so self-centred but resolved to learn from the recklessness.

After the gig, we went for a couple of drinks, still singing and dancing and (most likely) annoying everyone else in the bar. When it got to midnight, I decided it was probably time to leave for home. The boys wanted to stay, so I left them to it. They were doing shots as I put my coat on to leave, and I looked forward to hearing the rest of this story tomorrow morning.

I smiled and gave them each a hug. "Bye, guys. Have a good one!" I signalled the bartender to bring them two more shots before I spun to leave, shouting bye as I walked out the door and headed to the tube station. I felt the brisk wind on my face and hoped it would sober me up a bit on the way back.

Something didn't feel right. Out of the corner of my eye, I saw someone cross the road. I slowed down. This was my test to see if someone was following me. An ordinary person would keep going regardless of what I did, but as I listened to the footsteps behind me decelerate, the hairs on the back of my neck stood up.

I quickened my pace again and looked for the nearest crowded space. There was a bar with a smoking area out front about thirty yards away. I turned towards it. It took forever to get there. Once in front of the pub, I quickly turned to slot in sideways amongst the smokers, glancing back to see who was following me, but I only caught the back of a man turning and walking away.

My breath was shallow and rapid.

I recognised his broad shoulders immediately. His outline. Clad in all black. There was no doubt about it. He had been in our flat.

Now, he was following me home.

CHAPTER
6

T HE FRONT DESK had been quiet for two hours. The late January sun was shining, and there wasn't a rain cloud in sight. I was hardly surprised that people didn't want to spend their Saturday in a museum on a day like this when they could go for a crisp, winter walk in the park instead. I loved this weather. On my way to work that morning, I had enjoyed the air flooding my lungs with every breath and seen it plume out from my lips afterwards. People were actually sitting on street benches outside to eat their lunches, making the most of the short days to bask in the sun.

Leaning back in my chair, I thought about that night on the street after the gig. The dark figure had been playing on my mind a lot. Had he been following me or had I just been paranoid and a bit tipsy? He had looked so familiar, though. After the break-in, I wouldn't be completely insane to think that maybe I *was* being watched. Maybe someone knew about the unusual things I could do. But how? Apart from my mistake in the queue with the bouncer, no one should have any suspicions. Yet again I chose to push the subject to the back of my mind. I didn't like to think about it, probably because if someone else was aware, then I would have to deal with the reality of it being public knowledge. And I didn't want that.

I tapped my fingers on the desk and sighed theatrically. There still was not a soul around. The new work schedule allowed only one person on the desk at a time, so I had no one to talk to. The atmosphere at work had changed dramatically in the last couple of weeks, and I worried it was only going to get worse. Some of my favourite colleagues had been told they were no longer needed. The change in shift times had meant I was getting home later at night. The other evening, I didn't get home until eleven o'clock because there weren't enough people to help close up at the end of the day. I practically had to do everything by myself. I started tapping my fingers harder on the desk. Why was I doing more than one person's work at more unsociable hours for no increase in pay? Where was the logic in that? I huffed and shuffled in my seat, shifting my weight onto the other elbow. And all this in a toxic work environment where nobody was happy anymore.

A small group of people came through the door. I had to remember to perk up my face to greet them. Smiling brightly, I took their money, stamped their tickets and waved them through to the main entrance. Then,I slumped back into my chair. My phone was in front of me, and I skimmed through Twitter to see what was happening. If Jackie saw me, she'd be furious, but I'd stopped caring by that point. I wanted to see if anyone was up for meeting that Friday when I had the day off.

Drinks Fri nite? — Me

Yeah sure. Are we finally going to meet your new man? — Tash

Oooh yeah, bring him along! — Rafa

Ha, maybs! — Me

Amaaazing. George at 6 then — Tash

See you there — James

That was something to look forward to at least. I stared up at the darkening sky through the front window. People outside were looking colder now, doing their coats up to the very top buttons and burying their hands deep in their pockets. The sun was low and, with no clouds to hold the warmth of the day, it would be a chilly night. I peered back down at my phone and started tapping.

Hey Al. How ru? Fancy the pub Fri nite? Few m8s going. The George@6pm. Scar x

It had been a while since I'd seen Al, but I'd been so engrossed in reading and re-reading my new books that I hadn't had much time to meet him. Plus, I had to contend with my new work schedule. He was patient, though, and kept messaging to see if I might be free soon. I hoped he could come to meet everyone, if only so they would stop making imaginary boyfriend jokes.

My phone buzzed on the desk.

Good to hear from you! Sounds good. See you then ☺ *A x*

I was still baffled at how quickly he always replied, but I was hardly going to complain about that. I remember all too often waiting days for replies from guys I'd dated. I would check my phone constantly and take it everywhere with me. Once, I nearly dropped it down the toilet after balancing it on the edge of the sink while taking a shower. Looking back, I realised how ridiculous the whole thing was. Surely, if a guy doesn't get in touch, it's because he's not interested, so why would I want to hear from him anyway? Even when I was growing up, I worried that I wasn't doing things right. But I had no idea how things were supposed to be done. I felt this way about friends as well as boyfriends. It was confusing, and it made me insecure. Only with the combination of experience and hindsight could I look back and see how obvious it should have been. I thought about the people at school who would make me feel like I didn't matter, like the girls who wouldn't invite me to parties or would make fun of my clothes. As a result, I would dumb myself down and try not to stand out. I now know that it was their own insecurities making them act like that. I should have been more confident.

I thought about how it all sounded so cheesy. Even though girls were told this *all* the time by their parents, it still sounded ridiculous, and we refused to believe it. We were taught to be so self-critical that to be happy about ourselves felt arrogant. We ignored the advice and looked down on ourselves and wasted our time with people who didn't deserve our friendship.

Amber popped into my thoughts. As a young woman, I hoped Amber knew all of this. Maybe I'd mention it next time I saw her, which reminded me that I should visit her. This was the right term to go as she wasn't new anymore but also didn't have exams and projects to finish.

I picked up my phone again and started texting.

Hey Bams! Wan 2 c ur sister this term? Let me no wen is good.
Luv u! Scar x

"Hello?" I jumped in my chair and looked up. A young couple was standing at the front desk. It seemed I'd been ignoring them. I quickly put on my biggest smile, took their money, handed them two tickets and wished them a great visit. Once they had disappeared through the doors, I rested my elbow on the table and my chin in my palm, exhaling deeply. Maybe I should leave this job? I really wasn't enjoying it anymore, and hating a job is never good. I wished I had a book to read. That would be a great way to pass the hours. Maybe I should start looking for work elsewhere? Couldn't hurt to just see what else I could do.

I looked down at my desk at the museum-branded pen lying next to the keyboard. It started rolling slowly right to the stack of maps, clicking every time the pocket clip hit the desk. It stopped before rolling back to the keyboard. I'd become adept at the little magick things lately. When I was young, I had a knack for making stuff happen unintentionally, but doing things on purpose used to be tough. At this point, I was doing them out of boredom. The previous day, I had seen a guy coming out of the supermarket with a ready-made sandwich. Having taken the sandwich out, he dropped the wrapper on the ground and started walking away. The cardboard packaging lay in the middle of the pavement for somebody else to clean up. I don't know if it was my anger that made my intentions more powerful, but all I had to do was imagine him wracked with shame over dropping the litter. I watched as he turned around and went back to pick it up. I could feel the guilt easing away from him after that. The same thing happened when I was on the tube home after work. A pregnant woman was standing in the carriage of a packed train where no one was noticing her. She was obviously too polite to say anything despite the little button pinned to her coat saying, "Baby on Board." I was stood pushed up against the glass partition by a thirty-something with his headphones blaring. I looked at this uncomfortable woman and then at the healthy young professionals sitting down, ignoring her. I could feel the pain in her back, the ache in her feet. I broadcast her discomfort to the other passengers. I tried to act like an amplifier for her feelings, funnelling them into the faces of her surrounding passengers. Within moments, a few people cocked their heads up to look at her. Again, I could feel their remorse seep into the air. It wasn't long before she was offered a seat. I felt the relief rush through her as the weight transferred from her feet to the felt-covered seat cushion. She smiled with gratitude.

I thought back to when I was a kid and had no control over these powers. When I was ten, I sat in the doctor's waiting room, the clock ticking loudly on the wall and the receptionist shuffling papers endlessly. I looked at my mum who smiled down at me, but she smiled only with her mouth. Her eyes looked worried, and I was sad to think that maybe I was the reason for her anxiety. We were there because of what happened right after my grandad had died. My gran was heartbroken. He was the love of her life and her best friend. They'd met at "a dance" and had been inseparable ever since. And for the first time in decades she was going to have to learn to live without him.

I remember looking at her sitting alone after the service, gently weeping into her hanky, and going over to talk to her. "Grandad says you'll be fine." I looked up at her—an innocent child in a blue dress with yellow and while daisies on it—and held on to her arm.

She turned to me with a grateful smile and squeezed my hand. "Thank you, darling. He would say that, yes."

"No. I mean he says you were always the one in charge anyway, that you know how to run everything." I laughed and shook my head. "Grandad! He says now you'll know how little he really helped." I looked at my Gran to see if she was laughing at his joke, but her eyes had changed.

Her hand was still resting on my arm, but her grip had stiffened. "What do you mean, darling? When did he tell you that?" Her voice had changed too.

"He's telling me now!"

From then on, everyone was disturbed about the things Grandad had told me. I got the feeling that they didn't want to hear it even though I knew how much he wanted me to tell them. That was why I had to go to the doctor who asked me a lot of questions about "hearing things." I didn't like all the attention or the looks on people's faces when they talked to me about it, so I never mentioned it again.

I sobbed for days when Gran died. Sure, I was sad. But at the funeral she apologised to me. She was sorry she didn't believe me. I couldn't tell my mum, or she would make me go back to the doctor. Gran understood, though. She knew I couldn't tell them what she told me. I couldn't tell anyone. I think, after that, I eventually even convinced myself that I had imagined it all.

I wasn't that little, insecure girl any longer, realising now that I probably hadn't imagined a thing. Maybe my grandparents had wanted to send a message. Maybe that was the only time and only way they could communicate before they left for, well, wherever it was they had to go. Perhaps I was the only one who could hear them.

I looked down at my desk and noticed I'd been absent-mindedly tapping my pen against the keyboard. Blue ink had leaked everywhere. I didn't need this. Holding the pen perfectly still, I plucked a couple of tissues out of the box behind the computer and wiped my fingers, streaking navy blue across the tissue. However, the dark stain remained on my hands. I stood up to see who was around to watch the front desk while I went to the bathroom. There was no one, but I didn't see any visitors either, so I chanced it and went to clean myself up. Standing over the sink, the tap running, I looked at myself in the mirror. My eyes looked a darker, murkier green than usual. Odd. They were always so vivid. I turned my head down to the light blue froth swirling towards the plughole as I washed the ink from my hands. Taking a deep breath, I rested my palms on either side of the sink. When I had washed off as much of the ink as I could, I dried my hands on a paper towel and returned to my desk.

Jackie was waiting for me. "Scarlett, where were you? The front desk had nobody on it!" She was clearly unhappy. Her eyebrows were raised expectantly for my answer.

"Sorry, Jackie. My pen leaked, and no one was here to watch the desk while I went to wash it off." I raised my palms to show her the evidence.

"So, you didn't wait? You just left the desk empty? What if visitors had come in?" She crossed her arms tightly against her body.

She wasn't understanding what I was telling her.

"But nobody did! Did you want me to stay here and greet people covered in ink?" I felt my face flush with annoyance. My voice probably got a bit shrill. Jackie was a nice person, but she could give me a headache sometimes. We were stretched thin enough as it was, and now my manager wasn't even on my side.

"Scarlett, that's not an appropriate tone for the workplace. In future, please do not leave the front desk unless someone else is available to cover for you while you are away. Do you understand?"

My blood began to boil. She was treating me like a child because, if someone had come in, it would have reflected badly on *her*. Normally, she would have understood the situation. It was because of her own added stress and workload that she was behaving like this. I knew that, but it didn't stop me from being exasperated.

"I understand," I said through a clenched jaw. I stared at Jackie in the eye to show that she wasn't intimidating me.

Straightaway, she raised her fingers to her temple. Her face twisted in pain, and she pressed her eyes closed tightly. "Okay," she breathed the word more than said it. "Okay. Good. Wow. My head. This migraine . . . it came on fast. I need to get some painkillers. I'll speak to you later, Scarlett." She mumbled the last part as she had already begun walking away, her hand still cradling her head.

I sat back down in my seat. I was still agitated, but I was worried about what I had probably just done. Did I just give my boss a searing headache because I was angry with her? This wasn't like me. My anger dissolved into guilt. I wanted to apologise, but I what would I say? Sorry for making your head hurt? Instead, I decided to try to make it up to Jackie later by buying her a coffee or something. It seemed a feeble consolation, but I couldn't think what else to do. I didn't know how I'd managed to give her a migraine, so I wasn't sure how I'd go about taking it away.

My mind was whirring by that point, but in the background a decision was developing that would soon convince me that this job was over. I wasn't happy here anymore. I was starting to dislike myself. I didn't feel appreciated by my employers because they had me on a contract where they could "use me or lose me." And after that argument with Jackie, my roster was sure to be brutal. I thought quickly about whether I had the courage to quit this job. My frugal saving habits gave me enough in the bank to last a few weeks in rent and food. My heart started beating faster at the thought of it. I could really do it. I could quit this job and work somewhere else. I thought about the museum. I would miss it. It's not that I hated working in the museum, but I hated the situation I was in. The atmosphere was toxic, the contract was unstable and it was making me unhappy. I decided to sleep on the decision. If I still felt the same in the morning, I would hand in my notice. I got a surge of excitement mixed with fear. I worried about whether I would be able to find another job before money ran out, but I had to be brave. I had to change my path by force, or I would sit here miserably forever.

At home, Natasha had invited Rafael and James over and they'd ordered pizza for dinner. I was thrilled and felt like it was an appropriate celebration meal considering my big decision of the day. We drank wine, ate pizza and I told them all about the pen leaking, getting told off and how I'd just had enough.

"Oh, wow Scar, are you going to quit? For real?" Natasha looked wide eyed at me.

"Yep."

"Without another job ready to go to?" Rafael voiced the sensible side of me.

"Um. Yep."

"Well congratulations, Scarlett. That's a very bold move, and you know what? If it'll make you happy, then go for it." James was smiling at me.

"Thanks!" I took a bite of pizza so that they couldn't expect me to immediately answer any more questions. As I was chewing, I looked at my three friends. Natasha and Rafael were trying to suppress a look of concern and James looked overly happy. I started to wonder if I'd done the right thing. Why weren't they all happy for me? I had explained already about the change in hours, reduced staffing and everything else that upset me about the job. I decided to shrug it off. They were just being good friends and worrying about me.

Rafael cleared his throat and stood up. "Hey Scar, can I chat with you for a sec?"

"Er, sure." I put my plate down to one side and brushed the crumbs from my lap. Pushing myself up to my feet, I followed him to the kitchen. He circled around behind me to close the door. I asked if he was okay.

"Yeah, yeah, don't worry. I just wanted to check in with you since that guy followed you after the gig."

"Oh, right." My phone buzzed. It was Amber saying she'd love to have me up to see her A.S.A.P. I was excited to plan my visit and thought about going while I was temporarily "between jobs." I looked up to see Rafael's face staring at me.

"Have you seen him again? I'm just worried, with the break-in and now this. I didn't want to worry Natasha. I know she's still spooked."

"I haven't seen anyone else since then. Really, you needn't worry about me or Natasha." I gave him a hug to show him I was grateful for his concern.

"Okay, good." He mumbled, although he still seemed to be thinking about it. "And you're sure you're not quitting your job as a reaction to all this?"

"No, Rafa. It's because the place makes me miserable now."

He shrugged his shoulders apologetically. "Okay. I just wanted to be sure." He gave me a quick hug.

I felt we were being rude to the others, so I reopened the kitchen door with a cheery smile and went back to the living room. Natasha and James were talking about Friday and getting to meet Al.

"I'm not going to be able to come, after all," said James tilting his head and frowning, "I have to work late, and I'm up really early the next morning."

"That's okay! One less person to interrogate him." I narrowed my eyes at Natasha and Rafael accusingly, and they laughed back at me.

"We'll be good!" Sang Natasha.

"Promise!" Rafael chimed in.

"Yeah, you better be."

The next day, I walked into Jackie's office and handed her the letter saying I would no longer be available for any shifts at the museum. She was upset, but I had my suspicions that she was more worried about how she was going to manage with the gaps I would leave in her roster. I told her exactly what my reasons for leaving were in the hopes that honest feedback might improve things for the people who were staying, but I doubted she would take my suggestions seriously. I agreed to do the shift I was down for that day, but then I wouldn't be back. Walking out of her office, I felt liberated and happy and only ten-percent terrified, which was probably a pretty great balance considering I had just quashed my only source of income.

I spent the rest of the day in a good mood, although, when I checked around the exhibits that afternoon, I felt a pang of sadness. I looked at the Inca exhibit, and I felt the same wave of warmth and acceptance coming from the glass cabinets as always. Did I do the right thing? I loved parts of my job—especially being near fragments of history—but was it enough? I suppose I could always come back to see them, I'd just have to buy a ticket. The thought made me laugh. When the time came to leave at the end of my shift, with the few colleagues around who I felt a friendship with, I thanked Jackie for all the shifts she'd given me and left my pass in her office.

Esther, the tour guide, had a group of people waiting for her, but before I walked out the main doors, she ran over to give me a hug. "It won't be the same without you," I heard her say over my shoulder.

"Hey, good luck with everything okay?" I squeezed her back. "Take care," I said.

As Esther dashed back to her waiting guests, I pushed the glass doors open and walked out. As I turned towards the tube station, my eyes were distracted by a piece of paper stuck to a lamppost a few feet away from me. It was an advertisement for a job in a second-hand bookstore. "Ha!" I thought, reflecting on the coincidence.

I didn't think much of it after that, except for how wonderful it would be to work in a bookstore.

CHAPTER
7

WAKING UP WITH no job to go to was surreal. It was both liberating and terrifying. Exhilarating and intimidating. I decided to give myself a couple of days' breathing space before letting the true panic of unemployment really settle in. I meditated each morning in my pyjamas, calming the storm of uncertainty inside, before starting my day. I had started this habit in recent weeks, and I felt overall more together and peaceful because of it. I lit a yellow candle for inspiration and mental strength, focusing on ridding myself of dark thoughts. The air in my bedroom felt incredibly still, except for the golden flame that swayed hypnotically in front of me. The occasional car drove past outside. Conversations rose and fell as people walked by. I could feel the grey carpet underneath me as I sat on the floor. It pressed against the bare skin of my ankles, and the chill from the frosty morning air gave me a shiver. Every breath taken in was a cold flush to my lungs, infusing my blood cells and flooding my body with energy. With each exhalation, I puffed out uncertainty and fear. The dark cloud was filled with doubt and insecurity, but it evaporated into the cool, clear air, disappearing completely.

I kept thinking about the flyer on the lamppost outside work. The idea of being surrounded entirely by books *was* exciting. I wouldn't mind being engulfed in adventures and love stories filled with peril and victory. I thought about the journeys of self-discovery, of heroes and villains. I could live a hundred lifetimes just by reading books. People who never read would only ever know their own experiences. The tranquillity of working in a bookshop was seductive, too. I had always liked that about the museum. Although by the end it was the only thing I liked about working there. Worrisome, work-related thoughts started creeping into my mind, so I shook my head and my messy uncombed hair fell about my face. I didn't even know how old the flyer was. The job was probably gone already.

Natasha had left for work when I went downstairs for breakfast, so I sat alone in our quiet flat eating Cheerios. I thought about going to visit Amber on Saturday morning and what I would need to take. Going to visit her was an exciting prospect, especially since I could feel anxiety building around me here in London. A trip to Loughborough could be just what I needed to shake it off. The wall clock ticked loudly, and I could hear myself chewing the crunchy cereal.

I was completely alone in the flat. I looked at the radio and it clicked on to my favourite station. Smiling, I let go of my bowl. As if someone else was holding it, I watched the bowl float towards the sink. The tap turned on, and the bowl was rinsed and placed on the drying rack. In the meantime, the large, green sofa cushions had risen gracefully above my head and up to the ceiling. I watched as they circled rhythmically with the music. Delighted, I got up and danced along in my slippers and dressing gown, laughing at the lamp switching on and off and the books flapping open and closed. The copper candlesticks on the coffee table danced together while the coasters surrounding them did the hokey-cokey. The whole room was alive with movement and music, and I spun around in a circle until I felt my head go dizzy. The song that was blaring from the radio came to its dramatic end. On the final electrifying beat, I threw my hands up in the air and struck a ridiculous pose. After a beat, the living room fell back into place, and I collapsed, giggling, into the sofa.

As I came down from the shower, towel wrapped around me and my hair roughly dried, I walked into the living room on my way to the kitchen to make a cup of tea. Passing the sofa, I noticed the corner of a book poking out from under the big cushion. It wasn't a regular book, though. It was a notebook. I hadn't seen one like it since school, and I wondered why there was one stuffed in the sofa? I switched the kettle on and, while I waited for it to start bubbling, I pulled the rest of the book out from its hiding place. It was a regular green, lined exercise book with one word written on the front in capital letters:

NOTES—PRIVATE

I guessed it must be Natasha's. Was she working on a project or something? I always wondered how the organic food shop kept her interested, like she might be one of those literary geniuses who needed a humdrum job to create a masterpiece. But she had never mentioned any projects to me. I wondered whether I should open it. It felt like an intrusion, especially as it seemed to have been hidden away. But the intrigue began to overwhelm me. I would only take a little peek, I decided, to get the general gist of its purpose, and then slot it back into its home under the sofa cushion. The kettle clicked off as the bubbling noise subsided and steam wafted up from the spout, clinging to the window and condensing.

I looked around, even though I knew I was alone, and opened to the first page. It revealed only three words.

THINGS TO REPORT

What?

I was even more curious. Why on earth would Natasha need to report anything? And who is she reporting to?

I turned the next page. And the next. And the next. From then on, each page was filled with time codes and dates with cryptic notes written next to them.

"21.07 20:15 Cleanse"

"09.08 09:45 Minor use"

"13.09 15:30 Cleanse"

"04.10 12:30 Minor use, more sophisticated"

I recognised one of the dates as the night someone kicked in our front door.

"10.12 23:10 BREAK-IN"

The more I read, the less sense it made. I thought maybe it could be a record of things to report to the police after the break-in, but the dates ranged all the way back to last summer. I had no idea how I was going to mention this to Natasha. How do you ask someone about something you should never have been reading? A surge of guilt rose within me.

I closed the book and went back to the kitchen with my mind whirring. Stirring my tea, I stared out of the window trying to understand what it meant, but it was all too puzzling. Besides confused, I was ashamed that

I had read something which clearly had the word PRIVATE written across the front. And I felt ashamed about the things I was starting to suspect. Was Natasha crazy? Was she obsessed with something? What was she constantly monitoring? More importantly *who* was she constantly monitoring? I had always considered her a lovely girl. I appreciated the complete lack of drama about her, but maybe I had been wrong all this time. I wanted to go back and read the notebook more thoroughly, but I stopped myself. I had invaded her privacy enough. If she had wanted to tell me about what she was writing in that book, then she would have done so. I decided to leave it for now, and try to forget about it until she raised it herself. If she ever raised it. But my curiosity lingered in the back of my head.

To distract myself, I went for a walk. As soon as I stepped outside onto the top step of our stoop, I inhaled the familiar late morning smell of West London. It was a combination of fresh air that tasted almost like spring and the wafting spices from nearby street food vendors ready for the lunch rush. As I trotted down to the street and turned left to Portobello Road, the clattering of woks and pots grew louder and the smell grew stronger. Even though it was a weekday, there were always throngs of tourists lining the street shopping for antique knick-knacks or sitting and chatting outside while sipping coffee. People often asked me how I put up with the constant bustle of living near such a famous street. But I loved it. There was always energy in the air. It emanated from people who had travelled hundreds of miles to see London and had come to our little corner of the city.

I stopped by a delicious-smelling burrito stall staffed by a skinny guy in an apron ready to take my order. Looking at the menu board, I unzipped my purse and dug my fingers about for some coins or a note, but it was barren, save for a few pennies. I looked at my bankcard. I could hit a cash machine, but was I able to spend £7.50 on lunch while unemployed? I tried to do some quick maths in my head. I had six week's rent in my bank account but that's only if I spent absolutely nothing on food, drinks and bills. So, realistically, I had a month's rent in the bank. I worried that maybe four weeks wasn't enough time to get a new job. What if I ran out of money? I couldn't move back home to Bristol or ask my parents for a loan. As all this raced through my mind, I noticed a slip of purple paper flutter across my boots and the jangling of coins hitting the ground nearby. An outbreak of movement whipped up behind me as I scooped up the paper and inspected it. It was a £20 note. Behind me, a lady was collecting the contents of her purse that had spilled onto the floor. She was frantically scrabbling on the ground for notes and coins. Guiltily, I thought about how this simple piece of paper would allow me some of my old indulgences for a while. A few glasses of wine at the pub. A trip to the cinema. Maybe a burrito for lunch.

The man at the stall broke my concentration.

"Miss, did you want anything?" He sounded impatient. There were people waiting to order, and I was in the way.

I stared at the £20 note, aware that no one around had seen me retrieve it. The smell of the spiced meat swept over me. Hunger continued rumbling in my stomach.

"Miss?" He persisted.

My eyes lifted to meet his eyes. "Oh. No, thanks." I turned around and forced a smile. "Excuse me? I think you dropped this." The frantic woman looked up and enthusiastically thanked me for assisting her. Backing away from the stall, I headed home to make a sandwich.

After lunch, I decided to start job hunting online, searching first for something that might utilise my English degree. Nothing. With increasing desperation, I looked for absolutely anything within a commutable distance that I might be the slightest bit qualified for. It was a fruitless pursuit. Realising that this was how things were going to be until I found work again, the idea of celebrating and feeling of delight that I'd had that morning subsided completely. I was left with only fear, wondering whether I should go crawling to the museum to beg for my old job back. Taking a deep breath, I reminded myself that I knew quitting would be hard, and that I needed to have a bit more faith. Yes. Just a bit of faith. Everything would be fine.

I nearly had myself convinced.

The pub was packed with the clamorous Friday night "after work" crowd who were letting loose and laughing off the week's troubles. I had double-checked my makeup in the bathroom mirror and was happy with the outfit I'd chosen for when Al finally met my friends. I was clearly the most nervous out of everyone, constantly glancing at the time on my phone and taking big gulps of lime and soda as wine was temporarily unaffordable. For steadying the nerves, soda wasn't nearly as effective as wine. We were sat at the back again where it was possible to hear each other talk. Natasha and Rafael were seated opposite me. I made sure to have the chair facing the entrance, so I could see when Al arrived. There had already been several jokes, and they looked set to continue.

"Now would really be the time to admit he's not real," smirked Rafael, "although, if you really want to live in a Rom-Com, I'll give you ten minutes to find someone in here called Al to pretend to be your boyfriend for the night." He winked at me.

I kicked him under the table.

"Come on, Rafa." Natasha chimed in.

She would fight in my corner, surely.

"She doesn't need ten minutes. There's easily an Alex or an Alan in here, maybe even an Albert! Look I'll show you . . ." To my horror, Natasha rose to her feet and started yelling. "Al! AL! IS THERE ANYONE HERE CALLED AL?"

I yanked her back down into her seat by her arm. She landed with a bump, laughing hysterically with Rafael.

Then, I heard the looming figure next to our table speak.

"Um. Hi. I'm Al?"

My body froze. Only my eyes crept upwards, eventually landing on the familiar handsome features of the man that I'd met before Christmas.

Natasha and Rafael's mouths dropped. They were no longer contorted with laughter, but wide-eyed and motionless.

I stood up to greet our newcomer, giving him a kiss and taking him by the hand before introducing him to my suddenly mute companions. "Guys? This is Al." They continued to sit, staring at him, and I started getting a little embarrassed by it. "Al, Idiot Number One here is Rafa, and Idiot Number 2 here is my housemate, Tash. Once their brains re-engage, they will say hello I'm sure."

At this verbal nudge, they both stood up hastily. Rafael leant over to shake his hand vigorously, and Natasha kissed him hello on the cheek. They gradually returned to their old selves again.

"Sorry," Rafael apologised. "You see, we were so convinced you were fictional that it took a while to click."

"Oh, is that so! Well I'm definitely real. The Student Loans Company is more than aware of my existence, unfortunately."

Everyone laughed, and I was pleased that they did. We settled into the evening, and, when Al went up to the bar, I got a very excited but condensed debrief. They loved him as I knew they would. Natasha couldn't quite believe how stunning he was, which only mildly offended me. Rafael said he "seemed nice," which meant that he was being typically protective and reserving his opinion until he knew him better. This was good enough for me. The rest of the night flew by. Before I knew it, the bell was ringing for last orders. As we stood up to start piling on our coats and scarves, I turned to Al and summoned up some courage.

"You can stay at mine if you want? I don't live far." I turned to Natasha, who had started walking in the usual direction. "You go ahead, Tash!" I spun back round to Al and tried to act casual. He had never even been inside the front door, always waiting on the steps to pick me up. I hadn't thought too much about it until now, but I figured if he's met Natasha, it wouldn't be weird for them to bump into each other in the morning.

"I really can't," he said. "Sorry. Early start and all that. Can I borrow your phone quickly? I need to check the train times, and mine's out of battery."

"Sure! Of course!" I handed it over and carried on chatting about how we could grab breakfast the next morning before he left, but my persuasions fell on deaf ears. He held me by the shoulders and looked into my eyes.

"Your friends are great. I knew they would be. I'll see you soon, okay? Which way are you going? Down Portobello Road?"

"Yeah, same as always." I shrugged, trying—but probably failing—to seem nonchalant.

"And Natasha?"

"She'll be halfway back by now. I'll see her there."

"Okay, well take care." Al flashed one of his irresistible smiles.

We kissed, and Al walked away to go to Notting Hill Station. Rafael had already run to catch the night bus that was pulling up at the stop across the road. I looked back over my shoulder towards Al in the hopes he'd be looking, too, but I could just see the back of him. His hand was held up to his ear as if he was on the phone.

"That's odd." I thought.

Setting off on my own down the dimly lit road, I looked at the sleeping shops, so often alive with people. The market stalls were bare, metal cages without the wares of various tradespeople adorning them. I wondered what time in the morning they came to start setting up. There was no one else around, which was odd for a Friday night. I heard my own footsteps rhythmically tapping alongside me and thought about how well everyone had got on at the pub. I tried not to read too much into why Al wasn't keen to stay the night at mine. He had never invited me to his, either. Maybe he was an awkward sleeper and struggled to share a bed. Yeah, maybe that was it. He probably didn't want to keep me up all night by tossing and turning. Just as I was trying to convince myself that that was the reason, I heard a gruff question from behind me.

"Do you have the time?"

It was a man's voice.

Something in me clicked onto high alert.

As I turned around I felt a powerful, suffocating blow to my stomach. I shrieked in pain, my eyes snapped shut and all I could see was white. I doubled over. My brain tried to process what was happening. After a few seconds, clarity returned, and I straightened up to see the broad-shouldered man in front of me.

I recognised him immediately. He broke into our flat; I saw him my vision. He was also the man who followed me after the gig at Kings Cross.

It was painful to draw breath, and I felt a searing pain in my stomach. But I managed to crane my neck to look up. I saw his face.

He had dark brown eyes, almost black, with thick bushy eyebrows. His skin looked damaged by too much time in the sun. His chin was unshaven, and his head was completely bald.

I suddenly felt a surge of adrenaline. My attacker looked like he was taking his time stretching his fingers out. Maybe he thought he'd incapacitated me. So, I filled my lungs with air and stood up straight. Bending and lifting my right arm above my shoulder, I struck him in the side of the face by slicing my elbow across and into his left eye as hard as I could. I thought about my training and what my teachers had taught me over the past couple of years about being attacked.

The man barked in surprise and clutched at his temple with his left hand, so I quickly used my left elbow to strike him upwards to the chin. I knew I had the element of surprise. Whoever this monster was, he probably wasn't expecting me to fight back.

His neck arched backwards. He stumbled, hands cradling his head. He was looking up at the sky now, and I had my chance.

I focused all my energy into my right arm. With a clenched fist, I pulled back then thrust forward, jabbing my knuckles into his throat. My entire body weight had been behind it. The sound was like that of an airless splutter as my attacker reached up to hold his neck with both hands.

His eyes were bulging nearly out of his head. Blood trickled down the left side of his face.

I knew this was my opportunity to get away, but he was still standing.

Worried he would come after me, I knew I had to finish what he'd started.

I took my left foot and planted it so that I was standing only a couple of feet away from him. Summoning every ounce of my strength, I grabbed him behind the neck, interlocking my fingers. Our faces were only inches apart. I felt terror trying to take over my body, but I looked into his deep brown eyes and rammed my right knee squarely into his groin. I felt a sharp pain up my thigh from the sheer force of contact, but I remembered to jump back in case he swung at me. He collapsed onto the pavement wheezing in pain. His face was split open. His jaw hung ajar as blood dripped down his cheek and off his top lip.

I was panting heavily, still recovering from the punch to the stomach. The adrenaline continued to course through me. After a few moments, when I was certain he couldn't get up, I ran.

CHAPTER
8

T HE POLICE ASKED me the same questions over and over again. I heard my trembling voice recall what the man looked like, what he'd asked me, and any other details I could remember. I felt sick with the fear of what would have happened had I not been able to defend myself. All those hours of training had been worth it if only for this night. By the time I called the police, my attacker had disappeared, and there was no way to explain that he was the same man who broke into our flat. There had to be a way to convince the police that the two attacks were related. But I had no evidence. They'd never believe me. I never physically saw him in our flat and had no proof it was the same person. But it was worth mentioning that I had seen him following me home one night. So, I did. Then, they asked me why I hadn't reported it at the time. I never thought to report a guy following me unless he actually ended up hurting me in some way.

Eventually, around the same early hour as the night of the break-in, the police left, bestowing the same parting words of wisdom. "Call us the second you see him again."

"Of course. Thank you." By this point, even if he was a mile away minding his own business and posing no threat to me, I was going to call for help. He was now officially considered a dangerous stalker, and I had no desire to cross paths with him again.

Once the commotion of the evening had calmed down, Natasha made some tea and gave me some painkillers for the morning. "I thought you weren't coming back tonight?" She tilted her head to the side, her eyebrows furrowed.

"Well, I guess I was hoping maybe I'd go back to Al's, but he had an early start."

"Oh." I got the feeling she had another question but didn't want to push the issue.

"If he'd been walking with me, I bet this wouldn't have happened. I hate feeling like I can't walk alone at night." My eyes winced as I shifted in my seat to get comfortable. Natasha came over to help stuff a pillow behind my back.

"Are you in pain? Do you need to see a doctor?"

That seemed like an overreaction. I was severely winded and my stomach bruised, but I wasn't about to flat line. I thanked Natasha for all her worrying but declined the offer of a lift to the hospital. Instead, we sat for a while making small talk. I tried to hide the trembling of my hands as I sipped my tea. It was three o'clock in the morning when I eventually crawled upstairs to bed and tried to forget the whole night.

A few hours later, the phone alarm went off. I blearily silenced it, flinching in pain as I trudged through my morning routine. The grey London sky loomed over the city as people made their way to various weekend activities. The occasional drizzle of rain had umbrellas opening and closing like concertinas, and my Converse were soaking through as I splashed through puddles to Victoria Bus Station. Natasha had desperately tried to convince me to stay in London to recover properly— just until the shock wore off and I was feeling back to my normal self. She was unsuccessful. I had made plans to see Amber at university and, in my impoverished state, I found a way to go by bus for less than a tenner. This was vastly cheaper than taking the train, even though it would take twice as long. It was important I continue saving right now. Even Amber triple-checked I was still happy to visit after I told her a 'family-friendly' version of the attack. I did my best to convince everyone that what would make me happiest was to get out of the city and see my sister. Nervously, they all agreed.

On the bus ride up to Loughborough, I opened Whatsapp on my phone. There were already a number of messages asking about how I was. James was the first to message, which was odd for him because he was usually the last to find out about things. As Rafael found out, my phone started buzzing frantically.

I'm fine! Dn't worry! Going 2 c Amber now — Me

Scar! Why don't you move in with me? Then I could keep an eye on you! — Rafa

Don't b silly! Looked after myself didn't i?? — Me

That seems a bit dramatic. I'm sure you're fine at home, Scarlett — James

Seriously . . . I know you're capable but you're obviously not safe, Scar. Please, think about it? — Rafa

Going 2 read my bk now. 2hrs left on this bus! — Me

Always reading! You should work in a bookshop ☺ — James

I managed only about twenty minutes of sleep in the uncomfortable seat and spent the rest of the trip looking out the window at the concrete motorway and the passing cars. When I finally pulled into Ashby Road in Loughborough, Amber was waiting for me. I'd missed her wonderful, smiling face and leapt off the bus to give her a great big hug.

"Bamber! I'm so glad to see you. How are you?" I leant back to look at her properly before hugging her a second time. I hadn't quite realised how much I'd missed her.

"Hey, Scar," she laughed. "I'm okay, thanks. How are you? Feeling better?"

"Yeah, yeah. Don't worry about me!" She thought I'd been hassled by some late night drunk, not physically assaulted by a stalker. It seemed cruel to overly worry her. I bent over to pick up my backpack and felt a sharp pain from the bruise on my torso. I was only staying a night, but I never had figured out how to pack lightly. Luckily, it was only a short walk to Amber's campus accommodation.

"I've planned a quiet one tonight, considering everything that happened. I hope that's okay?"

We rounded the corner towards Telford Hall, and I took a deep breath of fresh non-London air, wincing again.

"It's the weekend, too, so we mostly don't go out anyway," Amber added.

"Fine by me." And it really was. All I wanted was some quality sister time.

Sitting on the sofa, I could smell the inviting aroma wafting through to the living room from the kitchen. Amber and her housemates had recently invested in a slow cooker and took turns each morning to prepare something and set it going. By the time they got home in the evening, dinner was practically ready. Amber had made an extra-large beef stew that morning, and I was looking forward to tucking in. When it was ready, we dipped our roughly torn chunks of French bread into the sauce and put a film on even though we knew we were going to end up chatting over it like we always did.

"So your course is going well?" I asked, a forkful of beef hovering over my bowl. I was waiting for it to cool slightly.

"Yep. Really enjoying it. I love being out on my own, actually." She smiled back at me.

"Ha. Don't let Mum hear you say that!" I poked her in the side with my elbow. "I loved my time at Leeds. I think you can really let go and be yourself at uni." Amber's eyes darted down to her bowl as she continued to eat.

I felt like I'd hit upon something. "How's it going with that guy you were texting at Christmas?" I tried to move the conversation on, and boy-chat was always a good way to get Natasha nattering away. Hopefully it would work with Amber.

"Who?" She looked up at me with narrow eyes before evidently remembering our conversation in her bedroom at home. "Oh. Yeah. That's still going well, thanks."

"I wonder if you'll ever bring him down to Bristol to meet Mum and Dad. That would be exciting! For me, I mean. It would be torture for you and, at best, uncomfortable for him." I nudged her with my foot teasingly and waited to see her reaction. She didn't laugh, or even smile. Amber's eyes were fixed on her bowl of stew. I asked her if everything was okay.

"Scar, you know how we talk a lot? How I like to tell you what's going on with me?"

I nodded, keeping my mouth shut so as not to interrupt her.

"Well, it's true that I have met someone." Amber placed her bowl down on the coffee table and turned to me. She looked me in the eye.

Her voice sounded rehearsed. "But it's not a boy. Her name is Jessica."

I carried on chewing the bread as I processed what she had just told me.

"Oh!" I exclaimed. "It's a girl? Oh, Amber. Why didn't you correct me at Christmas? I've been banging on about you seeing some guy. You should have said!" I put my bowl down on the coffee table, too. "You weren't worried about telling me, were you? You know it makes no difference to me." I smiled at her, my hand reaching out across the sofa towards hers. She didn't reach back, continuing to sit rigidly, her hands in her lap. I persisted. "It makes no difference to anyone anymore! Well, not to anyone worth knowing at least. I'm just happy you've met someone! Come on, Bams, this is great news. Can I see a picture?" I scooted my bum along the sofa so we were sat side by side, and Amber reluctantly got her phone out. I could see her physically relax now. Her stiff posture had slumped back into the sofa. Part of me felt sad that she had been worried at all.

Amber retrieved her phone from the bag by her feet, but, before she unlocked it, she turned to me, worried, again. "You won't tell Mum, will you?"

"Tell her what? I don't even know what's to tell. And surely that's for you to do? What exactly would you announce to her?"

"I don't know."

"Exactly. You don't have to put any labels on yourself. You don't have to announce you're gay, or bi, or anything really. You just be you." I put my arm around her and squeezed her shoulder.

"Thanks Scar." She hugged me back, then turned to look at me. "To be honest, I'm not totally sure that I *don't* like boys. I don't know if I *only* like girls. I just know that I like *this* girl."

"That's good enough for me! Now show me a picture and tell me about her. I'm dying to know more!" Amber laughed, and her face lit up as she began to recall her favourite things about Jessica.

For the rest of the night, we chatted away like we always did, and I felt like I had a little bit of home with me. I even managed to forget about the attack. Later that evening I was on the tattered old sofa with a duvet thrown over me. Lying there unable to sleep had given me time to think. Chatting with my sister reminded me how strong she is, how strong we both are. Neither of us fit the typical mold of "normal" in society. We hadn't chosen this path, and we felt we had to hide our true selves. But you can never be happy like that. Our situations were vastly different, but ultimately, we were both struggling with our identities.

The sofa springs were digging into my bruise, so I shifted onto my back and faced the ceiling illuminated by the yellow street lamp outside the window. I thought about running. I had run from my attacker and kept on running all the way up the country. But if this dangerous stalker wasn't going to stop chasing me, then I was going to have to go home and be ready for him next time. All this, and I had to find a job before money completely ran out. I groaned and shut my eyes, determined to stop worrying and, instead, enjoy the time I had left with my sister.

The next morning, I felt a whole lot better about things. Over breakfast, we planned our day: a scenic walk to the shops first, then lunch, then back to grab my bag before heading home again. It was a short visit, but I knew I had to go home and face reality. Loughborough was a wonderful place to venture around in the springtime. Amber showed me the Cedar tree in the middle of campus and the amusingly titled "Bastard Gates." There were plenty of parks in London, but I wasn't used to having so much greenery around. I loved it. At the side of the path was a rose bush, bare of any colour and weeks away from blooming. I bent over and breathed in the air around it, blowing it back out from deep within my lungs, bathing the plant in warm air. The corners of my mouth turned up as I saw the green stems spring to life and grow into a tiny, closed rose bud. Amber was busy replying to a text on her phone, so I took another deep inhalation through my nose and blew again onto the rosebud, watching the petals grow as it flourished into a deep pink rose. It was beautiful. I turned with a smile and skipped off to catch up with Amber.

We took a walk to a beautiful fountain outside one of the halls of residence before hitting the shops. Our venture around the retailers was mainly window-shopping with a stop off at the famous "Socks Statue." I loved the random art you found in city centres and we took a selfie with it to send to Mum. Then, we headed back to Amber's flat to gather my things for my trip home.

Back at the bus stop, I felt suitably refreshed to begin another uncomfortable journey home. I turned to Amber to say goodbye.

"Please come and visit me again sometime?" She pleaded. "When you're feeling a bit better and up for a big night out, okay?"

I gave her a big hug and promised I would. "You have to come visit me in London, too. As long as you don't mind a sleeping bag on the floor."

"Sounds good to me!"

I started to climb the steps into the coach, but before disappearing around the corner to my seat, I turned to my sister. "And let me know how it goes with Jessica!"

Amber laughed and waved me away to my seat before turning to head home.

I was so proud of her.

I used the long ride home to seriously think about things. There was a lot going on in my life right now. Even taking magick out of the equation, I had to find a new job and my relationship with Al wasn't stable. Most importantly, I had to worry about the constant threat from my violent stalker.

After coming to terms with the fact that someone was clearly after me, now I knew they actually wanted to hurt me. They knew I was different because the first incident was an attempt to stifle my abilities by hiding that crystal in my room. They managed to make me completely powerless and totally forget about my visions. I had been so consumed with figuring out who I really was and what I could really do, I didn't stop to think that maybe people out there might not be happy about it. Somehow, I had to try to continue with my normal routine of finding a job and living a drama-free life at home. And figuring out why someone had a vendetta against me. All this on top of what I didn't even want to consider: someone knows about my abilities. How many other people do? How soon until everyone does?

I started to think about Natasha and her notebook. Maybe she knew someone was stalking me and was trying to keep notes for the police? I was going to have to ask her when the time was right. But not just yet.

When I got home, I went straight to my room. It was late. I wasn't in the mood to be molly coddled by Natasha, so I slipped into my room making sure to take my shoes and coat in with me. I lay restlessly in bed, trying to keep my abundance of worries from whirling around in my brain again. Sitting up, I opened my laptop. The white glow of the screen lit up my face as I searched the job websites. I still found nothing that I was qualified for or that paid enough to cover my rent. After I had clicked on every suitable link I could find, I called it a night. Plugging the phone in to charge, I collapsed back onto my pillow and stared up at the ceiling, falling into a shallow sleep.

Over the next few weeks, I carried on trying to find work and stay sane. I started exercising by training in the park because money wasn't stretching to gym classes anymore. I spoke with every recruiter I could find in my area. Al was very understanding and, although I refused to let him pay for everything, he was happy to do various free activities around London. He told me he was still feeling guilty about not walking me home the night of the attack, and I could tell he was trying to make up for it. Going for drinks became going for lime and sodas. I had become an expert on which supermarket sold the cheapest instant noodles.

At least practicing magick was free, and I knew I had to get far more advanced if I was going to protect myself in the future. This focus was the only reason I was holding it all together. Concentrating on magick was the best way to stop myself from panicking about everything that had happened. I worked on the spells I had tried already and also managed to master some new techniques. Despite a lack of any formal training, I was doing quite well with spells by following my instincts—just as I had with the hot tea on my desk at home. I started to understand how the world fit together, and this helped me grow my magickal skills. Every spell was important even if I wasn't in any immediate danger.

One afternoon, bored and with nothing else to do, I went for another walk. I didn't usually go this far off the main road, but it was a refreshingly warm spring day. I had let myself wander further west than normal, along Elgin Crescent and up to Holland Park. After finding a cheap little café, I treated myself to a tea and read a book to distract myself. The walls were charmingly decorated with wanted ads. This was unusual for such an upmarket area, so I was pleased that the owner was helping the locals. I took another sip of my tea and peered over the top of my book, through the café window and out over the road. I saw a familiar logo on the shop opposite; it had a dark green background with gold-coloured writing. I tried to cast my mind back. Where had I seen that before?

Clattering the cup back onto the saucer without looking, I knocked the spoon onto the table. I leant forward and narrowed my eyes trying to get a better look at the sign.

EXODUS BOOKS Ltd 2218 Portland Rd

That's where I knew it from! It was the bookshop from the flyer outside the museum.

The shop front looked endearingly worn, the dark green enamel cracking up the columns on either side of the entrance. The window frames glinted in the sunlight as they were matched to the colour theme of the sign and slicked in a thick gold paint. A hip-height wooden bookshelf in the front overflowed with various hardbacks with cracked covers, and I could see more of the same inside.

Rising from my seat, I lifted my coat from the back of the chair and left a £2 coin on the table. I'm not sure I even broke eye contact with the shop front as I walked around the other tables and left the café, hearing the bell ring as the door shut behind me. I crossed the road and stepped into the open doorway, taking a tentative pause as I looked around. Inside, I could see flecks of dust floating in the light that streamed through the windows. I saw more books than I could read in a lifetime. They were piled and scattered about in a charmingly messy way. As I placed my finger on top of an old, leather-bound spine and pulled the book out from its shelf, I heard someone call from the back of the shop.

"Can I help you with anything, Miss?" came a disembodied voice.

"Hello?" I queried into the ether, stepping further inside. Slowly.

"Yes, Miss, can I help you?" It was a man's voice. Deep and sharp. A stark contrast to the surroundings.

I wandered between the rows of bookshelves in search of the source of the question. Something felt kind of eerie about the place, but part of me liked the sensation—like a haunted house. I turned the last corner to see a man sat at a large wooden desk covered with yet more books. He was writing in an open ledger, a calculator by his side.

I guessed he was the owner. "Oh, hello." I smiled politely. I felt I was disturbing him. "I was just having a look around."

"Of course." The man looked up at me.

I felt a chill snake down my neck. He was dressed in a sharp black suit with a crisp white shirt and a jet-black tie. He stuck out in this environment like a rock in a bowl of marbles. Scattered all around us were dusty, yet beautifully bound, books that appeared not to have been read in years.

I looked at him closer. His face was narrow. His chin and nose were pointed as if both had been pinched, and his dark hair was slicked back with too much product. I could smell his harsh and resinous cologne from a few feet away. My first thought was how the fumes were probably damaging the books.

I smiled warily at him and ventured a question. "Um, I think I saw a flyer about a job here. Is that right?"

The man stopped writing, put his pen down and leant back in his chair. There was a thin smile on his face. "Yes, I need some help. As you can see, I'm the only one here. The place is a mess. Are you interested?" His voiced was controlled, which was unusual for someone needing help because they were swamped.

"I might be. How much does it pay?" This could be a dream job if the money was good enough. The boss was a bit odd, but he probably wouldn't be around much.

"£9 an hour, 10am until 8pm."

I thought about it quickly. It was enough to pay the rent and have a bit left over. At this point, I couldn't be too picky. I would also save money on the tube since the shop was within walking distance of my flat. Plus, the consistent hours were better than at the museum. Having all those hours throughout the day to get lost in a book was a clear bonus.

I smiled at him and nodded my head. "Yes, I think that's okay for me. Do you want my CV and references? I can email them to you."

"That would be good. Thank you. Please, take my card." He slid the top desk drawer open, pulled out a simple white business card and handed it to me.

MATTHEW HOPKINS

Owner
Exodus Books Ltd

On the back were basic contact details, including phone number and email address. I tucked the card into my back pocket.

He rose to his feet to shake my hand. "I look forward to hearing from you soon. All being well, could you start on Monday?" He was leaning over his desk towards me, his eyes never breaking contact with mine.

"Sure, of course. Thank you for the opportunity." I unclenched my hand from his and started to leave. But before I did, I turned to ask him a question that had been playing on my mind since I'd seen the flyer. "Can I ask, why is this place called Exodus Books? It's not a religious bookshop, right?"

He paused briefly and looked down at his desk. Then, as if remembering himself, he laughed and shook his head as he answered. "It's a joke about books being on their way out. Internet and all that."

"Oh." It was an odd answer from the owner of a bookshop. "I don't think they are. I love books."

"Well, then you should definitely work here." And with that he sat back down, picked up his pen and went back to work.

It was difficult to know what to make of Matthew Hopkins. He was an odd character made even odder by the job he chose, but I soon forgot about him. I skipped my way home. I had a job again.

CHAPTER
9

"SCARLETT!"

"Yes, Mr Hopkins?" "I have to go out for a while. Mind the place for a couple of hours, okay?"

"Sure, okay."

"See the box of books by the front door?"

"Yes."

"Please go through them, note the titles and authors in the ledger, then put them out on the shelves."

"Okay, Mr Hopkins. I can do that."

Matthew Hopkins finally stamped his way down the wooden stairs from his office to the shop floor. I was sitting behind the large desk in the corner where I first met him four weeks ago, familiar now with what went where. Looking up at my boss, I saw his usual presentation: hair slicked back, crisp white shirt, black tie and trousers. We had spent a fair bit of time together over the last month. He was a curious man who took an interest in my home life and hobbies. He asked what my friends did for a living and how long I had been in London. He didn't have much to say about himself, but I figured he must not have led a very interesting life. I felt a certain amount of pity for him so, despite still giving me the creeps, I decided to give him the benefit of the doubt.

It had been a quiet morning, and our brief conversation was as much talking as I'd done all day. As he was putting on his jacket, Mr Hopkins bent over to pick up his briefcase. That's when I caught a quick glimpse of something unusual. At first, it looked like a smudge of ink behind his left ear. But it was too neat. He turned to me before I could get a better look. I thought it was odd. He didn't seem the kind to get a tattoo.

"Everything alright?" He asked as he saw my eyes narrowed and focused on his neck.

"Oh! No, no. Everything's good. You go. I'll be fine." I turned back to the desk where I had been cataloguing our stock of nonfiction and started counting the number of copies of each book we'd ordered. After a few seconds, the bell on the door rang as he left the shop, then the familiar sound of silence returned to the room.

I started thinking about tattoos, which got me thinking about Rafael again. He still hadn't messaged me back. It had been five days since his last attempt to get me to move in with him. I couldn't remember the last time we had gone so long without speaking. Before that, he had bought me something called a "defence spray," which would cover the attacker in a coloured dye that took a week to wash off. He said pepper spray was illegal in the UK, so this was the next best thing for catching the guy afterwards. They just had to look for a guy covered in bright blue dye. I felt safe knowing Rafael cared so much. He was like a big brother looking after me in the last few weeks. I had been much more cautious since the attack, taking more cabs home at night instead of walking and double-checking windows and doors before going to bed. Whenever we all met up at the pub, Rafael was always asking me if I'd seen anyone loitering or looking suspicious. It was actually starting to actively annoy James who maintained that Rafael was being over-the-top and ridiculous. James said it's a sad fact that people get attacked, but, "you have to move on with your life and stop being afraid." It's good advice, but James didn't know about the attacker being the same man who broke into our flat. Or the same man who followed me after the gig near Kings Cross. I had only told Rafael my hunch that it was the same guy every time and, being a good friend, he dutifully believed me.

But it had been five days since his last message. I hoped nothing serious was going on. I decided to wait until after work to go round to his flat and knock on the door. His housemates had never been particularly friendly, so I didn't have any of their numbers to call. But I was sure that a simple visit would clear the whole thing up. If he suddenly had to go home to Spain for a family emergency, his English number wouldn't be working, and he'd be much too distracted to worry about if I'd been texting him. His housemates would be able to tell me what was going on. I was sure of it.

As a distraction, I went through the books in the box by the door. It took about an hour and a half, but, eventually, they were all neatly shelved in their rightful places, filling the gaps their sold brothers and sisters had left. I went around the whole shop with a duster, trying to clean the place up a bit, but not enough to lose the charm of a second-hand bookshop. There were so many books I wanted to read: classics I had read before and looked forward to revisiting, and titles I had never heard of that promised adventure and mystery. I was making a mental reading list, but it was getting so long I figured I'd have to work twelve hours a day, seven days a week to get through them all.

Once the shop had been given a quick once-over and everything was as it should be, I went back to the desk and picked up my current novel. I had been reading it earlier when Mr Hopkins arrived for work, so it had been hastily slid it into a drawer. I'm sure he knew I spent a lot of time reading. There wasn't much else to do. But I didn't want him to see me constantly burying my nose between the pages of a book. This time, however, he'd be gone for at least a few hours. I could tell by the way he'd taken his briefcase and locked the office upstairs. I never heard the jangle of keys and the lock turning upstairs if he was only popping over the road for a coffee. Leaning back with my feet resting across the corner of the desk, I lost myself in another world for a while, safe in the knowledge the bell would alert to me to any entering customers.

About thirty minutes later, the bell rang. I shot up in my seat so I could attentively welcome the fellow book-lover.

But no one entered.

I was sure I had heard the bell, so I decided to venture to the front of the shop to see if someone had pushed open the door, and then decided not to come in.

But there was no one around. How odd.

I decided to think nothing of it and returned to my desk, picking up where I left off. After a few minutes, I was startled by a book falling from its shelf and onto the floor. I couldn't see where the noise had come from, so I wandered between the rows of shelves searching for the source.

Behind me, another book fell with a *thwack*. I turned instantly only to see it lying motionless on the hard wood floor.

Was I doing this? Was this one of those accidental times I was making things happen?

While pondering this theory, I took a few steps back the way I had come.

Thwack!

Right in front of me another book was pushed out from its cosy home on the shelf. This time there was a secondary noise. I listened closely, it happened again.

Meow.

I crept forward and looked in the bookshelf along the tops of the hardbacks. That's when I saw a little face staring back at me.

"Hello! Where did you come from?"

The face continued to stare.

"Was that you who rang the bell as you came in? That was very clever of you." I inched closer so as to not scare it off, but it didn't look afraid. I carried on talking in a gentle, friendly tone. "Who do you belong to? I don't blame you for coming here, but I don't think we have any books for cats. Although Alice in Wonderland has a Cheshire cat."

It meowed again and crept forward—towards me—looking for attention.

I put my hands on either side of its body, hooking my thumbs under the front legs, and picked it up. "You're a little girl cat! Well, how would you like to be my new colleague?" She clung on to me with her paws. "There are definitely a few mice around here to keep you busy." I smiled as I held her against my chest and heard her purring softly into my neck. After a few strokes and scratches under her chin, I put her down. While I tidied up the mess she had created to announce her arrival, the cat sniffed her way around all the shelves and boxes before exploring my desk and inspecting my bag.

I looked at the books she had knocked off. They were all of the same genre. "You're into your mystery thrillers then, aren't you?" I laughed.

She was a little calico cat, covered in patches of black, white and orange. Her nose was pink with a smudge of black across one side, and her eyes were a familiar bright green colour, which made me love her instantly. Picking her up again, I looked at her small, round face. "Hmm. No collar. What am I going to call you then?" I was answered with a blank stare. "I know! I'll call you Callie. Because you're a beautiful little calico." And with that, she meowed and jumped onto the desk to take a nap. As I settled back into my book, I thought about how nice it was to have some company.

Only a handful of customers came in that day, but I managed to sell them each a few more books than they had intended to buy. Finally, I could use my English degree for something. I could recommend several authors based on a customer's original choices, even offering to order titles in if we didn't have them. After every sale, I made a note in the ledger of the sale amount and the name of the books sold before putting the notes and coins away in the small money box locked in the drawer.

Mr Hopkins returned not long before we were due to close. But a few minutes before he arrived, Callie woke up and came to sit by me. When he finally came in, she ran and hid behind a box before dashing out the front door. Luckily, he had not seen her slip past him. I wondered if she would ever be back. Mr Hopkins seemed in a bad mood and clomped his way up the wooden staircase to his office. He unlocked his door and slammed it behind him. I never asked where he was going when he went out, mostly because I didn't care. But I wondered what he could be doing that sent him back with such a foul temperament.

It was eight o'clock. The end of my shift. I took his stormy entrance as my cue to leave. Shouting goodbye up the stairs and turning the sign on the front door to closed, I headed out.

Sitting on the tube, I waited patiently until the train arrived at Rafael's stop. I hadn't come here much before because of his weird flatmates, so I had to remember my way there by seeing what looked familiar. After a couple of wrong turns and retracing my steps, I eventually found my way to his doorstep. Rafael lived on a lovely tree lined street with what would have originally been enormous houses on either side of the road. But the street had gone the way of most of these streets in west London. Each multi-story home had been converted into several smaller flats, much like mine. Luckily there were only three flats in Rafael's building. I knew he lived on the top floor thanks to all the moaning about stairs he did.

I pressed the top button firmly and awaited a voice. Instead, the lock suddenly buzzed. I leapt to push open the door before the noise stopped.

After climbing three flights of stairs, I reached the top floor. Everything in the hallway looked a sickening yellow from the dim light of a single bulb hanging from the high ceiling. I knocked on the door. The girl who opened it the last time I visited Rafael stood there. She looked about as pleased to see me now as she had then. Her name was Greta. She was five-foot-two with short black hair and wide-set eyes. She reminded me of an eastern European grunge singer. With the attitude to match. I noticed Greta was already in her pyjamas. I wouldn't have guessed her sleepwear would be pink with little white rabbits. It was a comical contrast to her gothic makeup.

"Can I help you?" She instantly started rapping her fingernails on the door frame.

I forced a friendly smile, trying to warm her up. "Hi! I don't know if you remember me? I'm Rafa's friend, Scarlett?"

She looked me up and down. "Yeah, maybe. What do you want?"

"Well, I've been trying to get in touch with him for a while now, and he's not replying, so I wanted to check that he was okay."

"He's not here."

"Oh." I tried to peer over her shoulder into their flat, but she was blocking my view with the door only half-open. "Do you know when he'll be back?"

"No."

"Right." She wasn't being very helpful, but I continued to smile at her regardless. "Can you tell me when you last saw him?"

She sighed and turned her head inside towards the flat. "Hey! Michael!" I heard a faint shout come back from inside the flat. "When did you last see the Spanish guy?" She paused before shouting back again. "I don't care, but some girl is here looking for him! When did you see him?" Another pause. She turned to me—still waiting in the hallway—before answering.

"We haven't seen him since the weekend."

"But . . . that was a week ago. Have you tried getting in touch with him?"

"No. He's a grown man. He can do what he wants as long as he pays the rent."

My stomach flipped. The fears I'd hoped were unfounded were becoming real. I took out my phone and looked up the number for the branch of the restaurant where he worked.

"Are we done here?" Greta sighed her question.

"Yes. We're done." I said coldly, turning to put my phone up to my ear. I couldn't believe she thought I was wasting her time. She didn't even care that Rafael was missing. I was glad I didn't come round here more often.

By the time I got out the front door and back onto the street, the restaurant had confirmed he hadn't turned up to any of his shifts, either. They sounded pretty mad. I got the impression he might not have a job to go back to. Sitting on the steps outside his flat, I felt completely unsure of what to do next. Normally, I would call Rafael, and it pained me that I couldn't. I called Natasha instead, but she didn't answer.

After a few minute's thought, I decided to go to the police station and file a missing persons report. It felt dramatic, but Rafael wouldn't just disappear without telling anyone, especially me. Something was terribly wrong. After looking up the address of the nearest police station, I walked with such an urgency that I was practically running. Once I arrived, the desk sergeant watched me walk through the door.

I was panting and looking nervous. "I'd like to report someone missing, please." I rested my fingers on the edge of the counter top, feeling like a child in the face of authority.

"Okay, Miss. Just come through here and my colleague will take all the details from you. They've been missing more than twenty-four hours, have they?" She opened a door and led me through to an office.

"Yes. From what I can tell, it's been five days since anyone has seen or heard from him."

"Okay, then. You just sit here, and I'll send someone through. Can I get you a cup of tea?"

I nodded and looked around the room. It was so normal, like any corporate office rather than a crime fighting office of the London Metropolitan Police. Maybe I had watched too many TV shows about solving murders.

Murders. I didn't want to think about that. Why was I thinking about that? My brain always imagined the worst possible scenario in the hope that reality wouldn't be nearly as bad.

Just as my fears about what could have happened began to snowball, a kind-faced policeman sat down in front of me. He introduced himself as Detective Locke.

"So you say someone is missing?" The detective started tapping away on his keyboard, looking at the screen while I began to tell him everything I knew.

"Yes. His name is Rafael Cuevas García. I normally hear from him every day and his housemates haven't seen him and he hasn't been to work either." I struggled to still the tremor in my voice.

"Okay, just take your time. Write his address down for me here on this paper. Thank you. Is there any chance he could have gone home or away to visit anyone?"

"No, he was pretty broke after Christmas. And he's saving to go to a festival this summer." I was perched on the edge of my chair, squinting my eyes at the computer screen. My fingers gripped the wooden seat, whitening my knuckles, and my voice started to crack. "I'm sorry, I just know something's happened to him. Can you please start looking for him?" Tears began to well up in my eyes.

The detective continued to ask me questions about Rafael's habits and schedule until I felt I had relayed everything I had ever known about him. We finished and I left the station. The tears I had been holding in came rolling down my cheeks, and I gulped the cool night air. After a short while I began to calm down. I wiped my eyes with my sleeve.

The long walk home gave my fears time to fester. Eventually they morphed into resolution. By the time I walked through my front door, I was angry. I went upstairs and tried to do every spell I could think of that would help me locate Rafael.

Nothing worked.

I lit a purple candle for increased vision and enhanced intuition and settled on the floor of my room. I tried to see what he was seeing, but the screen behind my eyes where images had flashed before was blank. I tried to feel what he was feeling, but it felt empty. I tried to speak to him like I had spoken to Jet, but I ended up just silently shouting into the darkness. The flame from the candle burned tall and bright, but it was futile. It was like he didn't exist. The utterly unthinkable was starting to creep into my mind. I found a map of the London Underground that I had in my room and used it to show me where Rafael was in London, but nothing showed up. Nothing glowed or moved or gave the slightest hint that he might be in a particular area. I turned the map over to a broader map of the southeast train network on the back, but that was similarly useless. He was either much further away or . . .

I couldn't bear to think about it. I threw the map to one side and desperately tried to think of another way to find him. I came up with nothing. I sat on the floor with my back against my bed, exhausted. Empty. Tears blurred my vision. There was nothing I could do but wait and hope the police had better luck than I did. For what felt like hours, I continued to sit, hoping a brilliant idea would strike. It never did. Eventually, the night began to fade into morning. I drifted into a hollow sleep while leaning against my bed, my shoes still on my feet and a stream of dried mascara down my cheek.

A few hours later, I woke up to the sound of people outside busily going about their morning. I could hear Natasha downstairs in the kitchen having breakfast before work. For a few moments, I got to live without the worry that my friend was missing. The memory of the night before quickly dawned, and I felt sick to my stomach. After wiping my eyes, I stretched my legs out. They were sore from sleeping uncomfortably. I hobbled along the hallway and down the stairs towards the sound of morning television and found Natasha sitting in the living room eating her cereal.

She turned to me, her eyes wide and her spoon suspended before her open mouth. "Are you okay, Scar? You look terrible!"

"No one has seen Rafa." I collapsed onto the sofa. My eyes were stinging from lack of sleep. I felt cold.

"What do you mean? Who did you ask?" Natasha stopped eating and put the cereal bowl down on the coffee table.

"I went to ask his horrible flatmates, you know, the ones we met at the housewarming? They haven't seen him for days. I rang the tapas restaurant, and he hasn't turned up for any of his shifts either."

Natasha leant forward, her eyes darting back and forth as her brain searched for ideas. "What can we do? How are we going to find him?" Her voice was understandably frantic.

I was too tired for her panicked energy to be infectious. I felt drained and answered her wearily. "I filed a missing persons report last night. The police know he's gone. They have his home address and his work address. I can't do any more than that."

I thought about my failed attempts at magick from the night before and felt useless. I had yet to fail at something when I really put my mind to it, but finding Rafael was just a step too far for me. I was an amateur. When my friend really needed my help, I couldn't be there for him. Tears started trickling down my cheeks again.

Natasha's demeanour softened, and she came over to comfort me. "Don't cry, Scarlett. If the police know, then they'll be out looking for him. You can rest now. You've done your bit. I'm sure he'll turn up totally fine." She didn't look like she believed herself, but I appreciated her saying it for my benefit.

Looking at her through my watery eyes, I decided to take a chance and ask Natasha a question I'd been dying to ask for weeks. "Hey, Tash? There's something I was wondering . . ."

She stopped hugging me and leant back to look at my face. "Yeah?"

"I hope you don't think I was snooping or anything, but I found your notebook. The one under the sofa." I could feel her arms around me tense up.

"Oh."

"I'm so sorry. I know it said 'private' on the front, but I had a look inside, and I just wanted to know what you're writing in it. I'm so curious. Of course, you don't have to tell me . . ." I was hoping she didn't call my bluff and take the easy way out.

She looked awkward and went to sit back down on the other sofa.

The silence was proving too uncomfortable for me to bear, so I carried on talking. "I mean . . . it looks like you're monitoring something?"

"Um, I suppose so." Natasha shifted in her seat before springing out of it. "Look, I don't really have time to talk about this. Can we do it later? I really need to get to work." She hastily put her bowl in the sink, grabbed her coat and slipped her shoes on.

"Oh, okay," I mumbled as I watched her speed around the room. I must have crossed a line. She didn't want to talk about it. That's alright. Maybe in the future she would open up to me about it.

Right before she left, Natasha turned to me from the front door and softened her voice again. "Try not to worry about Rafa. You know he's a smart guy. He'll be fine. The police will probably find he's flown back to Spain last minute or something. If I hear anything from him, I'll let you know." And with that, she disappeared out the door.

My phone began to buzz. I pulled it out of my pocket to see who was calling. It was Al. I wasn't in the mood to talk to him right now. Despite everything going well between us for months, he still refused to stay over at mine. I was starting to find it annoying. I rejected the call, and let the phone drop into my lap. It was only eight o'clock and there were a couple more hours until I had to be at work, so I let myself drift into a shallow, unsettled sleep. When the alarm finally went off on my phone, I woke up feeling like a zombie. Putting my coat back on, I simply grabbed my bag and walked to work without changing my clothes.

Not a lot happened the rest of that day, except Mr Hopkins seemed in a better mood than usual.

CHAPTER 10

A THIN BEAM of dusty, speckled light fell through the shop window
onto the floor beside me, landing a few feet to the left of where Callie
was lying down for her afternoon nap. Normally, she spent her time
scrabbling around the floor catching spiders. She was a true master of pest
control. I watched her dozing peacefully, noticing her little twitches. I
liked to imagine her dreaming about catching mice and birds.

My body was tired and aching from lack of sleep. I sat staring at the
patchwork of colours on her fur as her little ribs rose and fell with each
tiny breath. It felt comforting to know this small creature had no worries
in the world right now. No police calling to ask more questions. No phone
to constantly check for updates. No deep sense of loss or fear that
something terrible might have happened to someone she loved. She just
lay there blissfully slumbering the afternoon away, oblivious to all the
terrible things going on in the world.

I lifted my gaze from the sleeping feline and looked around. The shop
was still in disarray from yesterday's customers leafing through various
novels before leaving them haphazardly misplaced. I usually enjoyed
reorganising in the morning before we opened, but I just didn't have the
energy. Ten days with no word from Rafael. The police seemed to have
no clues as to where he could be. His family were worried sick. I couldn't
imagine being called by the police to ask if I knew where my son or
brother was. Once, during my time at university, my phone broke on a

night out. My mum nearly boarded the next train to Leeds to find out if I was okay. I know if anything ever happened to Amber, I'd be hysterical.

We had put notices in the local paper and around west London asking if anybody had seen Rafael or anything suspicious near his flat around the time he disappeared. So far, no one had come forward. His mum, Isabel, had got in touch a few days ago to ask me for a recent photo of him. I couldn't help but crumble into tears. She sounded so brave, but I could tell it was all a show. This whole time she had tried to maintain her composure—a façade of bravery and determination—but I was sure that, when she was alone, she was crying much more than I was.

Natasha had been kind and comforting—as well as strangely distracted—since I told her the news. She always had something prepared for dinner when I got home and the washing-up was quickly done before I had a chance to get to it. She would listen to me worry as I posited theories, nodding her head and making me feel like, just maybe, he could still turn up. But then she would spend ages on the phone in her room, leaving me with far too much time on my own to think.

Yesterday, while sitting on the sofa alone in our living room, I hastily shoved my hand under the cushion to see if the notebook was still there. It wasn't. I don't know what I was expecting. Maybe to see if she had mentioned Rafael in her notes? I wasn't about to find out.

I felt desolate. Lost.

At work, Mr Hopkins was still acting strange compared to the first few weeks I'd worked for him. His concern for my missing friend seemed disingenuous. But maybe I was misreading him. I knew very little, if anything, about him apart from the fact he was a bit odd, so I didn't think too much about it. I just sat behind my desk, doing my best to greet the customers cheerily and as if I wasn't entirely consumed with despair.

James had met up with Natasha and me a couple of times since Rafael's disappearance. He seemed to have accepted the unthinkable. I found it hard to be around him. I still believed my friend was alive somewhere, in trouble maybe, but alive. James spoke as if we should be mourning. Al was no better, telling me I needed to accept what was happening and start to grieve for my friend. I supposed that those who knew him best were desperate to believe he was okay, and those who weren't as close to Rafael had a more pragmatic view of the situation. Rafael had been gone for nearly two weeks. I couldn't imagine a scenario where, after that kind of time, he would reappear unharmed with an innocent explanation for all the confusion.

Surrounded by stacks of books I sighed deeply and tried to put off the feeling that I was about to descend into tears again by holding my head in my hands. I saw the fluffy patchwork approach me, and Callie jumped onto my lap. She purred and rubbed herself against my cheek. Immediately, I felt comforted. Her green eyes looked up at me, and she slowly blinked before going back to nuzzling her face into my neck.

A piercing ring cut into the air abruptly, but it wasn't the shop phone; it was mine in my coat pocket. I held Callie on my lap as I shuffled to retrieve the ringing phone from my coat. Looking at the screen, I could see the detective's number.

"Hello, Detective Locke?" Without meaning to, I'd filled my voice with hope. "Do you have any news? Why are you calling?"

"Yes, hello Scarlett. I just wanted to give you a call about a recent development."

My heart was in my mouth. Had they found a body? My worst fears rushed to the front of my mind. "What is it?"

"Well, we found Rafael's phone. It had been knocked under his bed at his flat. Luckily, like most people, his pass code was the same as the bank PIN he'd written on an old statement so it was easy to crack."

"Detective, please. What is it?"

"Yes, okay. Sorry. There was a message he typed out on the night he disappeared. He must not have been able to press send for some reason. I was hoping you could make sense of the message," he paused briefly, "as it was meant for you."

I struggled to breathe. *I* was the last person Rafael had tried to communicate with before he disappeared? Why hadn't he taken his phone? Rafael always had his phone, which means he had probably not gone willingly. I guessed the Detective would have also known this.

"What did it say?" My voice sounded small. I was afraid to know the answer but, at the same time, was desperate for any new information.

"I'll text it over to you so you can have a look. Please think about what it could mean, and let us know immediately if you come up with anything."

"Okay. Thank you, Detective."

I hung up the phone, placed it on the desk in front of me and waited. After a couple of agonisingly silent minutes, it buzzed. A message came up on the screen.

Detective Locke—It read:

> *"Named I'd bit tour fried, ve fateful"* Please let us know if this means anything to you. Regards. Det Locke

I stared blankly at the screen until it went to sleep. I lit it up again, only to continue gazing hopelessly at it. How could this be the only clue as to his whereabouts? The message made no sense whatsoever. The excitement that had surged only moments earlier faded back to all too familiar despair. I slumped back in my chair and sobbed.

After work, my eyes red and aching, I packed my things away and headed for home. As I opened the door to leave, Callie darted off to wherever her real home was. I put my headphones in my ears and went on my way. I often listened to music when I walked, but now I rarely walked without it. My mind wandered too easily in the silence, and it always ventured to the darkest corners of my thoughts. I didn't want to think anymore. I had imagined every possible scenario, good and bad, and it was starting to become apparent that the worst outcome might be never knowing what happened to Rafael.

I was walking past some large white houses, most of which had not been divided into smaller flats, all of which were luxuriously decorated from what I could glimpse through the large bay windows, when I felt a presence behind me. Or, I should clarify, I felt a persistent presence behind me. I hurried around the corner, taking the long way home to avoid leading a potential attacker to my front door, but the presence kept pace with me. It was dusk and the streetlights were starting to flicker on. I steadied my breathing as I struggled to deal with the fact I may be about to get attacked again. I had been worrying about this constantly since it happened that night after the pub and had always had my wits about me. But this was the first time that I genuinely felt another threat from being followed. The idea of using magick flitted across my thoughts, but I knew that had to be a last resort, especially out here in the open. I shuffled past the flower shop on the corner and decided it was time to stop running. I could handle myself; I proved it last time.

With a quick spin, I turned my back to the wall and waited for whomever it was to walk straight into me. The sound of my heart drummed in my ears. I felt a tingling sensation as adrenaline started to flush through me when a small figure in a dark jacket rounded the corner into my path. I lunged aggressively forward, grabbing them by the collar and turning with force into the wall.

"WHY ARE YOU FOLLOWING ME?" I shouted hysterically, my grip tight and my voice cracking. I was surprised at the lightness of the person I was holding down. They were shorter than I was, and the build was all wrong for a man. I focused and looked up from my hands, noticing the long hair falling to either side of their shoulders. I followed it up to a young, frightened face staring at me with wide, brown eyes and trembling lips. Letting go, I pushed myself away from her and removed my headphones so I could hear her answer.

"I . . . I'm . . . I'm sorry." She quivered, clutching a notebook to her chest.

"Who the hell are you?" I demanded. I started pacing back and forth, letting the adrenaline ease off, trying to clear my head.

She was clearly shaken. The woman rearranged her jacket and smoothed down her dark brown hair. She was wearing professional, yet sensible, clothing and had a navy-blue handbag over one shoulder. I repeated my question impatiently.

"Sorry! I'm sorry. I didn't mean to alarm you. I tried shouting, but you didn't answer me. You're Scarlett Gardner, right?"

"Yes. Why? Why are you following me?"

"I'm Rose. I work for the *West London Herald*. I'm writing an article on the disappearance of a local man by the name of Rafael Cuevas García. I understand you knew him?"

"I *know* him, yes." I corrected her. I ran my fingers through my hair and scratched my head. She was a reporter. She was doing a story on Rafael, and she wanted to get my heartbroken statement so she could include it in her story.

"Please, if you could just tell me a bit about him, if you think maybe he was in some kind of trouble? Even just tell me how much you miss him?" She flipped open her notebook and slid a pen from within the ring binding, poised to scribble once I started talking.

I wasn't about to be quoted in the local press describing how tortured I felt at the disappearance of my friend. I walked up to her and calmly assured her I was not interested. "It's in the hands of the police. Please leave me alone." And I turned to walk away.

"Please," she protested. "It's important to keep the community updated on potential dangers in the neighbourhood!" But I had already put my headphones back in, drowning her voice into nothing. I carried on home.

A couple of miserable weeks later, I sat in the living room with Natasha discussing honestly how we were feeling. Up until then, any mention of Rafael made me clam up. I had been looking for any kind of distraction to avoid the inevitable conversation, but the time had come. We both knew that the police were most likely now looking for a body. We both knew that, as much as we had loved our friend, caring and worrying mattered for nothing in the search to find out what happened to him. Slowly, the realisation loomed that we were going to have to come to terms with what had happened, even if we didn't know exactly what that was.

"Maybe we could have a . . . a small funeral service. Just us. For Rafa?" Natasha suggested tentatively.

I looked at her with watery eyes and mindlessly clutched at the cushion on my lap. "That sounds so final."

"I know. But . . . You have to accept something before you can start dealing with it. I . . . I think we have to accept he's not coming back."

"Oh, Tash. Sometimes I don't think I can take any of this. I feel like I'm starting to crack." My palms were pressed firmly against my forehead. I felt Natasha sit herself next to me, resting her arm around my shoulders and pulling me closer. Her voice became calm and soothing.

"Let me tell you something. We all suffer through life. None of us is an impenetrable wall of perfection. These cracks, they represent our history."

"They're so painful," I whispered.

"Yes, but it's through the cracks that we experience the world."

I hadn't seen this side of Natasha before. I stayed silent for a while, absorbing her words.

She was right. It hurt because it was real. I knew I couldn't wallow in uncertainty forever. Reluctantly, I agreed to Natasha's plan for a small, informal ceremony. There didn't seem to be any point in waiting. Later that evening, we gathered together all the things that reminded us of Rafael, including stories about him, and we poured our hearts out. The room was lit with candles. I had downloaded music by his favourite Spanish band and played it in the background. Initially there were a lot of tears, but once they dried up, we laughed about how funny he could be. We spoke about his kindness and his generosity and how much he would be missed. After about half an hour, we ended by describing the many ways in which he was one of the best people we had ever known. How our lives were deeply richer having been his friend. Once we had packed everything away again, I felt different. Not lighter, but not chained down, either. A part of me was sad that he hadn't come to speak to me, like my grandparents had at their funerals. Maybe because the ceremony was so low-key, it may not have counted somehow.

I rang Al to let him know what we'd done.

"Has it made you feel better?"

"It has, actually. I'd rather be happy remembering what an incredible person he was than be constantly miserable that he isn't around."

"I guess so. Well, I'm glad you're moving on, anyway. What are you up to tomorrow and Saturday?"

"No plans. Will just be at home."

"Well, that's not right. I'm going to take you away on a break. You deserve one after all you've been through. Let me make some plans, and I'll come pick you up in the morning."

"Are you serious?" A smile spread across my face as I thought about getting away from everything and spending some quality time with Al. I hadn't been in the mood for company for the last few weeks, so we had only been texting occasionally.

"Of course, I am. Be ready bright and early. I'll pick you up at nine o'clock. Pack overnight stuff."

"That's amazing. Okay, well I better get to sleep then. Thank you, Al. I really appreciate it."

"My pleasure."

Before going to bed, I threw a few essentials into a bag: a smart change of clothes, makeup, toiletries and so on. I had never been taken on a surprise trip away anywhere, especially not with a boyfriend. I agreed that some time away from everything that reminded me of Rafael might be good for me, and good for us as a couple, too. For the first time in ages, I didn't fall asleep wracked with sorrow.

The next morning, Al turned up right on time and waited on the front steps while I finished getting my things together. Natasha wasn't up yet, so I tried to be quiet as I tip-toed around the corridor outside her room. I asked where we were going, and Al said that he knew a nice little B&B in Surrey with acres of gardens around it where we could have long walks and enjoy the fresh air. I was pleased that he knew me well enough to appreciate that this was the perfect break. I Googled the place we were going to so I could make sure I'd packed the right things. It looked wonderful.

"Right! I'm ready to go!" I handed Al my overnight bag, which he carried to the car, and I started to put my coat on. Natasha still hadn't woken up, so I scribbled her a quick note.

> Gone for the night with Al to a B&B to get some fresh air. Not sure about phone signal there so if you need me call The Bramble Hatch on 01784 555 190.
> Love, Scarlett x

I could hear my name being called from outside, so I hastily left the message on the coffee table and rushed out the door. In the car, we passed the time chatting about unimportant things. We hadn't seen each other in a while, so there was plenty to talk about. I told him all about my new job at the bookshop and about my weird boss. Al thought I was being silly about getting the creeps from Mr Hopkins, saying that he was probably just a normal guy looking after a struggling business. Could that explain his peculiarity? Looking after a shop that isn't doing well is probably quite stressful. I also rattled on a lot about Callie, the cat, and what a great companion she was and how she liked to push books off shelves. I told him about how she always seemed to know when the boss was coming back, which was handy if I'd got lost in a book. Al clearly wasn't a cat person. He said she sounded annoying, and referred to Callie as a "mangy street cat." I would've been hurt if he wasn't completely wrong. I assured him she was beautiful and funny and extremely good company.

We stopped at a petrol station to fill up the car. While Al went inside to pay, I looked over at his phone stuck to the dashboard with the SatNav displayed. I noticed the tab titled "View Total Journey" in the corner. Al had always been so vague about where he lived and always had an excuse for why I couldn't go to his place. Maybe his phone would show where he came from before he picked me up? I knew it was wrong to look through someone else's phone, but I had the chance to find out a bit more about him and felt I had to take it. I was his girlfriend after all. It was laughable that I didn't know where he lived. A cursory glance towards the shop confirmed he was still standing in the queue waiting to pay, so I quickly leant over and hit the tab in the corner of the screen. It showed a larger map of London with a purple line travelling from north London down through the west side of town where I lived, then heading off south out past Heathrow and on to Surrey. I dragged my fingertip across the screen to centralise the starting point and zoomed-in several times until a single house in Camden was on the screen. The purple line started bluntly in the driveway. So, that was it. He lived on Chalk Farm Road. I wondered why he'd never taken me there. Men were seemingly more and more cagey when it came to dating online, so perhaps he had been burned by a crazy ex and didn't want to reveal too much. It hit me that maybe I was doing something similarly crazy and felt ashamed of snooping.

A nearby car door slamming shut shook my train of thought off the tracks. I looked up to see Al coming out of the sliding doors, busy putting coins and the receipt in his wallet. I quickly hit the "View Journey Directions" tab. The screen reverted to show us as a blue arrow sat at the petrol station. I slid back to my seat. We continued on as normal, the guilt of my snooping slowly fading. It turned mostly to a feeling of reassurance that I now knew something else about Al. Something real.

We arrived at the magnificent B&B in the countryside after a couple of hours of trying to get through the polluted London traffic. The place was exactly as it had looked online. A wall of patchwork reds made up the colourful bricks on the outside. The rose bushes out in front were perfectly preened. Fallen leaves were scattered up the gravel driveway. The interior was all dark, varnished wooden floors and low ceiling beams. I squeezed Al's hand as we carried on looking around. Out the back was a well-worn cobblestone path winding between beautifully manicured hedges eventually stopping at the foot of a bridge leading over a lake. The wooden arch had creeping bougainvillea in a vibrant magenta along the sides, reminding me of the flowers we had at home climbing up the side of the house.

We walked over the bridge and out onto the grass amongst the trees for an hour before having the picnic lunch we had brought with us. For the first time in a while, I felt happy. Sitting under an oak tree, we nibbled on Scotch eggs, potato salad and fresh French bread from the supermarket unglamorously tipped out onto paper plates. The prosecco wasn't quite cold, but we didn't care. It was a light spring day, and we toasted to the good things in life outweighing the bad. I silently toasted to Rafael and hoped that he was at peace now. The bubbles felt good as they burst in my mouth. We sat for ages drinking, chatting and watching the occasional deer wander past grazing on the grass.

We spent the rest of the day goofing around. In the evening, we ventured to a small Italian restaurant a few streets away. It was recommended to us by the owner of the B&B as a "quiet and romantic" place. It was perfect. The candles flickered on the table between us. The gentle guitar music in the background was authentic and enchanting. The food was rich and delicious, and the wine went down all too easily. I looked across to Al who was breaking off a chunk of breadstick with his perfectly white teeth and telling me about a place he'd been to in Naples that had the best pizza he's ever tasted. We'd had a wonderful day and it was exactly what I needed. I felt as if I'd done something for *me* after weeks of worrying about someone else.

As I excused myself to the ladies, I asked Al to order me another glass of wine. I looked in the bathroom mirror, took out the expensive Tom Ford lipstick I only kept for special occasions and reapplied it. Then, I lightly dusted my t-zone with powder to get rid of some shine. I went to check my phone but realised it was still in the car from when we arrived at the B&B. Surprised at how long I had gone without thinking to look at it, I delighted in the fact that I had been having such a good time. Finally,

I smoothed down my purple dress, tussled my hair in the mirror and went back to the table to find a full glass of wine waiting for me.

"Perfect timing." Al beamed. "It's just arrived."

"Lovely!" I took a big sip from the glass. It tasted different. "Did you order the same kind? The pinot noir?"

"I think so. Sorry if I got the wrong one. Is it okay?"

"Of course, it is." I felt silly for being difficult. "It's fine, thank you." I returned to my carbonara and was about to comment on how good it was when I overheard a frantic conversation coming from the front of the restaurant. I looked over and was stunned to see Natasha talking to the manager, who promptly looked in our direction and pointed to our table.

"Scarlett!" she shouted.

"Oh my god, it's Natasha! What's she doing here?"

Al's eyes sharpened as he turned around to see my flatmate at the front of the restaurant.

"Sorry, but I need to find out what's wrong." I scraped my chair back and hurried over to where she was standing.

"Come outside with me, please." Her voice was low and serious.

"Tash, why? What's going on?"

She pulled me by my sleeve out onto the street.

"How did you find me?"

"I got your note on the coffee table. The owner of the hotel said you were here."

"What's happened? Why are you here?"

"Look, trust me when I say you need to come home with me. Please, Scarlett, it's very important."

"Are you crazy? I'm having a wonderful time. This is the first time in *months* I've felt happy!"

"I know that's what you think, but you have to believe me when I say this is serious."

Natasha looked at me in a way that I couldn't quite work out. It was a look of concern mixed with panic. I struggled to understand what had brought it on.

"Tash, go home. I'm fine. Al is here with me, and we're totally fine." I turned to go back inside. I was annoyed. She had no right to disrupt my romantic getaway with my boyfriend. Was she jealous? No, she'd never acted like this around him before. Maybe I was right when I found her notebook and thought she might be crazy. Didn't matter anyway, I was going to resume my date with Al and forget she ever turned up.

I wove my way back through the tables to where I had been sitting— and where Al was patiently waiting—to try to salvage the evening. Natasha remained standing outside for a while, talking on the phone, before she finally disappeared. I apologised to Al profusely. He was equally alarmed and suspicious as to why she had burst in like that. I assured him that, although I had no idea what was wrong, it was nothing to worry about.

After dessert, we paid the bill, which I insisted on splitting as he had paid for the B&B. I stood to put my coat on and staggered slightly to one side. That was odd. I had only had two glasses of wine, yet I felt distinctly unsteady on my feet. I took a deep breath in and held onto the back of my chair before standing up straight again. I headed for the door. When I got outside, the fresh air helped only slightly. I felt increasingly dizzy. The feeling only got worse as we carried on walking.

We were just arriving at the driveway of the B&B when I felt a nauseating wave come over me. I stumbled forward, tripping over my own feet and falling onto my knees. The gravel from the driveway was digging into my palms as I stayed on all fours trying to work out what was happening, but I wasn't thinking straight. My eyesight started drifting left and right, in and out of focus, disorientating and confusing me.

I expected to feel Al trying to help me up. But . . . nothing.

My head started hurting. I lifted my gravel-stuck hand up to my temple. I thought I heard Natasha's voice again, but it was hard to tell from the deafening pain in my head. I could definitely hear shouting between a man and a woman.

Crawling forward, I tried to get to the front door to look for help. I only managed a few feet before collapsing face-first into the ground. As I slowly drifted out of consciousness, I could feel the ground pressing into my cheek. I listened hard for any clue as to what was going on.

No more voices. No more shouting.

I summoned the strength to open my eyes one last time, looking sideways along the gravelled ground.

Nothing but darkness.

As I let my heavy eyelids fall shut, I could hear the sound of crunching coming towards me.

Footsteps.

Then nothing.

CHAPTER
II

T HE POUNDING IN my head wrenched me out of a darkness I didn't
recognise as sleep. Before even opening my eyes, I could feel every
muscle aching. My tendons were frozen and stiff. My mouth was dry, and
I felt nauseated. My eyelids, too thin to block out enough light, flickered
open warily before automatically squeezing shut again.

I rolled painfully onto my side. Fragments of the night before were
slowly trying to piece themselves together in my head, but the jagged
edges weren't fitting into each other. A bitter taste lingered on my tongue
as I licked my dry lips. I was desperate for water. As I pushed up onto my
left elbow with my right hand shading my eyes, I felt a stabbing pain
through my stomach. My eyes blinked open again. The familiar sight
around me gradually came into focus: the grey carpet, purple curtains, the
desk covered in books. I was in my room. On the nightstand next to me
was a glass of water, some painkillers and two slices of cold, buttered
toast. This had "Natasha" written all over it. I needed to speak to her to
find out what happened. She must know something if she put me to bed.
I gingerly swivelled my aching legs out of the bed and onto the floor to
steady myself enough for a drink and a couple of tablets. I would let these
kick in before going to find her. When I did, she offered little in the way
of explanation.

"You just found me drunk?" I rasped, making sure I understood her
correctly.

"Yes. Here on the front steps. I think you fell over and decided to just stay there. Had to drag you inside to bed." Natasha was busying herself putting laundry in the machine. And avoiding eye contact.

I was instantly suspicious, but then I hadn't any better suggestions as to what happened either. The last thing I remembered was our small ceremony for Rafael. "I don't understand." Slumped into the kitchen chair with my head cradled in my hands, elbows on the table, I tried to will my memory to kick into action. What explained the cuts to my palms and knees? But nothing surfaced.

Natasha left and came back with the plate of toast from my room and placed it in front of me. "Eat something."

"Don't want to." My voice came out muffled through my fingers. I wasn't sure I would keep toast down right now and didn't want to risk it.

Natasha had moved to the sink. The rattling of the plates hurt my head. I rubbed my eyes, still sensitive to the morning light, and contemplated my options. Still tired, I went back to bed. Resolving to write this day off, I hoped when I felt better it would all come back to me. Whatever 'it' was. Drinking too much was out of character. I'd never lost an entire day from memory before, but since Rafael had gone, I'd not been feeling myself. Maybe this was a result of sorrows being thoroughly drowned. Back in my room, I closed the curtains, crawled back under the duvet and didn't emerge until the next morning.

As I left the house, the looming threat of rain kept the skies dark and the birds hushed. The air smelled wet. I expected a storm was approaching. Heading off to work, I opted to take the long way round. The walk would stretch out my still-aching muscles, and the time to think would clear my head. Wandering past the new houses, I tried to remember what had happened a couple of nights earlier, but that whole chunk of memory was still inaccessible. There wasn't a single hazy glimpse or sound bite that hadn't been wiped out. The sensation of peering into the darkness—trying to see something where there was no light—reminded me of when I was attempting to locate Rafael. I tried to see through his eyes or feel through his fingertips and had come up with nothing. It was surreal to look into a part of yourself and see nihility.

As I walked along, I hoisted my jeans further up around my waist, tightening my belt another notch. The stresses of the last few weeks had taken their toll in a variety of ways. I rounded the corner from one street onto another with identical Victorian houses along tree-lined pavements and checked my phone to make sure I was still going in the right direction. I had wandered slightly off course, but it wasn't a problem. Another left at the next set of lights and it was a straight line to the bookshop, albeit from the opposite direction than usual. A growl of thunder echoed around the bruised clouds, and I clutched at the umbrella in my bag, ready for a sudden rain shower. It was only another ten-minute walk at most. I was nearly on the last straight towards work. I circled the pub on the corner with the hanging purple and white flower baskets dangling overhead, and then I turned left at the junction.

A few feet farther, I stopped dead.

My breath caught in my throat. I nearly choked. It took a split-second to process the scene before I dove, panicked, into the pub doorway.

I replayed the flickering picture of what I'd just seen. Incredible but definitely real. Mr Hopkins and Al were roughly twenty feet away on the corner of the next set of traffic lights. Together. They were together and in conversation, because it appeared Mr Hopkins was angry at Al. My boss was shouting at my boyfriend! I struggled to think of a reasonable scenario where they knew each other, but I couldn't figure out what connected them . . . besides me.

I leant out around the big wooden pub door frame, squinting to see what was going on, but the conversation had finished. Al was walking quickly towards me with a furious look on his face. Leaping back into the safety of the pub, I waited, body and mind frozen, until he walked past. Once the footsteps and indecipherable angry muttering had died out, I looked back down the street.

Al was gone.

In the other direction, I could see Mr Hopkins heading to the bookshop.

Shit, I thought. *I have to go to work.* I had no idea what had just happened, but I had to go to work or it would look suspicious. Calming myself with a few measured breaths, I carried on to the bookshop. It was only a couple of hundred meters, but when I arrived, the heavens had opened. I was soaking wet.

"Scarlett! Good lord, you're drenched!" Mr Hopkins had his coat on and was holding his briefcase when I entered.

"It's raining," I said, at a loss for any other words. After the shock of what I'd seen, I had completely forgotten to get my umbrella out. I could feel the rain soaking through my shoes.

"Well, I can see that. Bring an umbrella next time."

"Okay."

"Anyway, I just dropped in to pick something up, but I have to rush back to the bank. Good thing I've got this!" He brandished a large, expensive red umbrella at me before leaving. As the door swung shut behind him, Callie nipped in out of the rain and started meowing at me. I got the hand towel from the bathroom to dry her off.

My mind was racing, trying to figure out any kind of connection between my boss and my boyfriend, but I was awkwardly getting head-butted in the shins.

"Meow."

"I know, I know. Hang on I'll get you dry."

She was staring at me with those large green eyes and dark, pooled pupils, her whiskers twitching. I thought about how I never brought Al to work where he could have met Mr Hopkins. I never introduced them.

"Meow."

"You're chatty today, aren't you?"

"Meow. Meow. Meow." She was up on her hind legs, front paws dirtying up my jeans. I finished by wiping her paws on the cloth.

"Okay. There. Done. Now, off you go." She darted towards the bottom of the staircase and stopped abruptly to turn and look at me. She continued to talk at me. Chirping. I was sensing an odd urgency in her tone, then felt ridiculous for thinking that was possible. Then again, I communicated with Jet when I was at home. The dog and I had "connected" that day on the hill, but I was only giving him commands. I never heard anything back. It was like he was receptive to me but unable to reply. Why did I feel like I could understand Callie? She continued noisily at the foot of the steps to the office, and I struggled to think properly about whether Al and I had ever bumped into Mr Hopkins when we were out on a date.

"Meow."

"What do you want?"

I marched over to her as if expecting an answer when Callie excitedly started up the stairs, halting abruptly halfway to turn to check I was following her. I dragged my aching limbs up the steps behind her as she nimbly sprinted the rest of the way and stopped short of the office door.

"Meow."

"Do you want me to go in the office?"

"Meow."

"You could be a bit more helpful than just 'meow,' you know."

She rose up on her back legs and started scratching at Mr Hopkins's door up towards the round, brass doorknob. Rattling the handle confirmed what I already knew: Mr Hopkins locked the door whenever he was out for more than a few minutes. Rubbing herself against my legs in a figure of eight, Callie seemed to be urging me on.

There was no one around. I wondered if I could just slide the lock mechanism over one turn. The old-fashioned doorknob with the keyhole in the middle of the brass handle looked simple enough to unlock. It was surprisingly easy to will the components to turn.

The old door creaked open eerily.

Callie raced into the office and jumped on the desk. She started sniffing files and papers. I gingerly stepped one foot inside, knowing I was betraying Mr Hopkins's trust. But I felt there was something in there I had to find—something that might explain everything that had happened in the last few months.

I looked around the dimly lit, dusty room. The blinds were pulled down over the large back window. A sleepy moth was flickering sporadically, trapped between the glass pane and unfolded linen. There was a dark, oversized mahogany writing desk in the middle of the space. Behind it was a matching chair covered in a dark red leather seating pad. Switching on the dirty ceiling light revealed little more except the names of the books on the shelves. Nothing really stood out. It was mostly overflow from downstairs, duplicates and so on.

Callie was sitting on the desk chair, one orange and white paw on the handle on the top drawer in front of her. She clawed at it in vain, unable to move the heavy, timber tray. She continued to meow at me. As I crept over, she jumped from the chair to the desk and turned to observe me. I pulled on the brass handle of the drawer Callie had been so interested in.

The drawer slid open easily. Inside was an array of typical desk detritus. Pens and pencils. Tippex and highlighters.

But there was something I didn't expect to find.

In the centre sat a book. I'd meticulously catalogued every book in the shop and never seen this one before. It had a large navy-blue leather case with gold writing on the front. Around the outside of the cover was an ornate pattern in similar gold stitching. The book was rather beautiful. The writing looked like Latin and was clearly legible despite the fancy script.

Malleus Maleficarum

Hesitantly, I reached down to pick up the hardback and inspect it further. It felt heavy in my hand. The cover was rough on my fingertips. The title intrigued me. I didn't know much Latin, but I knew the first word meant a hammer of some kind. I remembered from GCSE biology that there is a hammer shaped bone in the ear called a "malleus." The second word oozed negativity from the root. I could feel it in my stomach.

Unnerved, I sat on Mr Hopkins's chair and opened the book to leaf through the pages. Each turn prolonging my confusion. It was written in old-fashioned English, with lengthy, drawn-out sentences that took ages to get to the point. But the sentiment was clear. At first, I thought it was a religious text full of prayers and sermons. But there was a specific word that caught my eye too many times—a word that appeared so much that, clearly, this was the theme of the book.

"Sorceress"

The more I frantically searched through the delicate paper pages, the more I noticed certain words.

"Witchcraft."

"Evil."

"Torture."

"Confession."

I gasped for air. I had been holding my breath.

This was because of me. This book was in this draw because of me.

The weak light in the room strained my eyes. I felt a sick, dizzying feeling, reminding me of the barbaric blow to the stomach I'd suffered weeks earlier. I brought one hand up to my middle, remembering the pain, remembering the man who had tried to hurt me.

I knew I had to get out of this office. Mr Hopkins could be back any moment, and it was dawning on me that I was in more danger than I realised. Grasping at my phone, I snapped photos of the pages that looked most relevant to me before shoving the tome back in its place and slamming the desk drawer shut. Callie rushed out between my feet, and the door banged shut behind me. It locked almost automatically with just a flash of instruction. I swept downstairs to grab my bag and coat and get the hell out of there. I would make up an excuse for why I had to go later, but, for now, I knew I had to leave before Mr Hopkins came back.

Outside, it was still pouring. I placed a fidgety Callie down under the shelter of the doorway whispering, "Sorry, girl" before running off through the rain. My aching muscles were fuelled with adrenaline now. I couldn't feel the pain anymore. To avoid bumping into anyone I knew, I rushed home a different way without stopping. I flew up the steps to my flat and clumsily shoved my front door key into the lock before scaling the stairs to my room. Panting from the surging adrenaline and the sprint home, I paced around my room, dripping wet, clutching my head, searching the walls at a loss for anywhere else to find answers.

This was too much of a coincidence. I squeezed my eyes shut and tried to restore some order, but the frantic memories from twenty minutes ago hopping around my head were hard to pin down. I couldn't look at them properly. Jittering snapshots out of order were flashing up, and they weren't making any sense.

A list would help. I would list the things I'd seen that day in order. First, I'd seen Al and Mr Hopkins arguing with each other. There was no way I could figure out how they would have come to meet. I was the only connecting factor between them as far as I was aware. I thought about how I got the job. A flyer outside the museum. Could that have been placed there specifically for me? I remembered other snippets from conversations about how my love of books meant I should work in a bookshop. Was it all planned? Who had mentioned it? I couldn't remember. Connecting with anyone online was already a risky way to meet people. With no mutual friends to vouch for Al, I simply trusted him from the start. Why? Because of his looks. Plus, he was so charming that the sceptical, wary side of me had gone straight out the window. I was ashamed of myself for being so superficial. Had Al targeted me? My feelings for him, which had been so strong and honest, suddenly soured. I reflected on his interest in my life. Perhaps it wasn't my sparkling wit that he was attracted to. Maybe he was researching me?

I was calling everything around me into question. A wave of nausea forced me to the bathroom. It was too much to take in. My support structure was caving in, and a feeling of wretched loneliness was filling my bones.

I looked in the mirror as I rinsed my mouth in the sink. My mascara had run down my face, and my normally full, wavy hair was wet and matted. The person staring back at me was thin, her face grey and tired. I was worn out.

Spitting into the basin, I noticed the other toothbrush on the side. And the yellow loofah on the shelf next to the coconut scented moisturiser. Natasha's things were everywhere. Natasha. Who was she before I met her? It was impossible to know. She had answered an online ad for the spare room and, ever since, she had been living in the next room aware of my every movement. The notebook. I thought about the notebook I found under the sofa cushions. What had it said again? The exact entries were hazy. Some kind of monitoring, reporting, times and dates with notes and comments scribbled next to them. Was I *her* subject, not Al's? Natasha had become one of my best friends. The thought of her betraying me like this was painful. Part of me refused to believe I had been living with some kind of secret agent for a year. She had always been so kind and understanding. Then, I remembered Natasha finding the crystal in my room and throwing it away. *Wait a minute. Was she on my side or not?*

The confusion became overwhelming. I rushed back to my room and locked the door. The rain continued to hammer down outside, each raindrop hitting the window with force before trickling down with the others. I had become side-tracked from the list. So, Al and Mr Hopkins know each other. What next? The book in the office drawer. I took my phone out and looked at the photos of various pages. They were blurred by my hasty snapping. Only a few lines were legible, but they nudged the memory of what I'd read. I swiped across to the picture of the book cover and Googled the Latin title.

There it was: *The Witches Hammer.*

I felt the world stop. I wanted the world to stop. I needed time to understand what I was dealing with.

Quietness crept into my room, bringing with it a stillness I hadn't yet experienced. The usual sound of ticking from the bedside table alarm clock was absent. I sat in silence waiting for everything to catch up with me. My room lay in a deep quiescence. I couldn't hear a single noise, even from outside, and stood up to see what was happening. Had the rain finally stopped? Astonished, I stared out the window at millions of static raindrops suspended in the air. Each tiny crystal droplet hung motionless, poised to continue. I saw the leaves in the trees rigid and the birds overhead paralyzed mid-flight.

Down below, I could see a black, orange and white figure sitting on the front steps. How had Callie found me here? This cat was definitely special—not just any old stray. I went downstairs to let her in. The scene in front of me when I opened the door was even more spectacular than it had been at the window. I could see people down the street holding their position as if they were about to start filming a movie, waiting for someone to shout "Action!"

The silence was overwhelming. I knocked on the wooden door to assure myself I hadn't gone deaf. Callie sat lifeless in front of me. Kneeling to her level, I looked at every seemingly frozen hair on her coat. Her whiskers stood perfectly still. Callie's neck was craned away from me looking along the street.

I lifted my eyes to the sky full of hanging raindrops. Focusing my dwindling energy, I gave them a mental kick downwards in the hopes of getting everything going again. Like yanking on a lawnmower chain, the clattering of rainfall burst through the silence, startling me into stumbling backwards. Callie turned to see the door open and ran inside out of the storm and up the stairs. I took a moment to consider the magnitude of what had just happened. I had accidentally stopped time. Without even intending to, I had stopped the entire world for a few minutes and, as far as I could tell, nobody had the slightest idea it had happened. Glancing back out the door, I saw people continue on as usual. Surely, panic would have ensued had they realised what just happened? The implications of this ability were staggering, but exhaustion was crawling further into me as the day went on. This last exercise had drained me substantially. Back in my room, I lay on the bed and stared at the ceiling, Callie hopped up and lay next to me on my pillow, purring. Her fur was wet and her paws muddy, but I didn't care.

"Why do I feel like you know what's going on?" I said to her little round face.

She whimpered back at me and shuffled closer.

Sighing, I continued to think about the book. Essentially, it was about finding witches, but the worrisome part was how they determined who was and wasn't a witch. Most tests involved innocent people dying and guilty witches surviving long enough to be hanged. The more I thought about it, the more it seemed savage and archaic. Could witch hunting still be happening in the twenty-first century? Maybe Mr Hopkins had the book for another reason? I had to find out.

The only way to go about this was to stop being on the back foot. No one knew that I had seen Al and Mr Hopkins talking in the street. No one knew that I had seen the book in the office drawer.

Looking at my phone again, I saw two missed calls from work. Clearly, my absence from work had been noticed. I texted Mr Hopkins's mobile number.

So sorry, not feeling well. Will let you know when I'm better.
Scarlett

It was a terrible excuse, but it would have to do. I opened the last text from Al. It was funny and seemingly genuine, and was yet another rejection to me going round to his place.

A glimmer of a memory crept into my mind. I knew where he lived. I thought about Chalk Farm Road and the purple line on the SatNav. I thought about sitting at the petrol station. But where were we going?

Of course, the B&B!

Bit by bit, the perfect day we had spent together pieced itself back together in my mind's eye. I remembered everything.

Except how it ended.

I needed to use what little information I had carefully. I had the upper hand and it would be foolish to waste it. As far as anyone knew, nothing had changed. I had to keep acting normally.

Callie had curled up at the bottom of my bed and was fast asleep, her whiskers twitching again. I fell asleep next to her, desperate for the rest. Around five o'clock that evening, I headed to the gym to train. It was a great way to clear my head and to feel stronger, which was seriously necessary at a time like this. I thought about the night I was attacked on Portobello Road, and how this training saved me. From what exactly, I had no idea. But I knew I had to keep getting stronger. I couldn't rely on anyone else to keep me safe right now. Not the police. Not my boyfriend. I had to be enough.

Stopping time was a huge step forward for me, but I had done it accidentally. This was the kind of thing that needed to be controlled and manipulated.

When I got home, I found Natasha sitting on the sofa eating dinner, the TV blaring in the background. She looked up welcomingly, but before she could speak, I dumped my gym bag in the living room and dashed upstairs to my room. I wasn't ready to confront Natasha yet. Despite the millions of questions that I had for her, I had to figure out if she was on my side or not. Until I knew for sure, I couldn't risk letting slip that I knew something was going on.

A plan started formulating in my head. I texted Amber.

Urgent! Can u & Jess get a train dn 2 Ldn 2moro? Scar x

I knew she would come. We always had a "no questions asked" policy in the case of emergencies; this fell precisely under that banner. The adrenaline in my blood had worn off, and sleep began seeping slowly under my eyelids. As Callie sat on the window sill, framed by the moonlight, I slid under the duvet into bed and drifted off to restless sleep.

CHAPTER 12

THE WIND BLEW a strand of hair into my eyes prompting me to pull it back behind my ear. Leant against the bright red post box, I tried to look casual. But on a residential street, I felt conspicuous and loud. The sun had already risen, and most people were heading out to work, heads down while on their phones, scuttling to the nearest tube station.

I had overdressed. It was warm for this time of day, and I felt hot in this black duffle coat. My frayed nerves felt trapped underneath the downy padding. I took big gulps of air to calm down as smartly dressed commuters rushed by, ignoring me. Reaching again into my pocket to check the time on my phone, I peered around the pillar towards the house—the house where the purple line started. I could see the silver car we'd taken to the beautiful bed and breakfast parked outside, and I knew this was the right place.

Just as I put it back in my pocket, my phone buzzed. There were two unread messages. The first was from Amber.

On the midday train down, see you soon. Amber x

The second was from Natasha.

Hey Scar! Haven't seen you in a while, just want to check everything's okay? Let me know if you need to chat, I can cook dinner tonight if you like. Xxx

A door slammed not far from me. I looked up. There he was. I eyed him turning to lock the door before dropping the key into his pocket and ruffling his thick, dark brown hair. Swinging back around, Al trotted down the steps and out the front gate. I had tactically positioned myself on the opposite side of the house from the tube station to ensure he that wouldn't have to walk past me. Sure enough, he turned away and strode off down the street. I knew I had to wait a few minutes to give him time to get down the road and turn the corner, so I got my phone back out.

Natasha's message seemed sincere. She sounded like the same old Natasha I'd always lived with, caring and considerate. I replied saying a chat would be good, but with Amber visiting, we'd have to postpone dinner. Sliding the phone back into my pocket, I quickly crept along from my hiding spot and up the same pathway that Al had just left. A cursory glance around revealed no one paying any attention, so I pressed my ear up against the coffee-coloured door, listening to determine if there was anyone else inside. No movement. No sound of murmuring. Only silence. I placed my hand over the lock and slowly twisted my palm anti-clockwise, bringing the deadbolt with it. Then, I raised my palm to do the same to the rim-latch lock at the top. The wooden door creaked open. I slid inside noiselessly before gently clicking it shut behind me.

I noticed the smell first. The wave of his cologne brought me right back to that wonderful first date in the wine bar. His perfect smile flashed across my closed eyes and feelings of fondness were beginning to creep their way back into me. Our romantic kiss in the snow played out in my head. Then, I remembered his clandestine meeting yesterday. My feeling of fondness darkened; it was turning to grief over the man I'd lost. He was gone. The trusting man I thought I knew never existed.

Opening my eyes, I saw a normal home. Probably identical to the many other terraced houses on this road, complete with inoffensive wallpaper, IKEA furniture and flat screen TV. I trod lightly towards the kitchen to look around, but it appeared similarly void of personality.

Something struck me as odd.

I realised that there were no pictures hanging on the walls. Or propped up in frames on tables. Nor were there any bookshelves, much less books, to put on them. It was a house with no memories or character, just a shell with bare necessities.

Edging closer to the stairs, I stayed alert to the prospect that someone could still be home. The banister took most of my weight as I tip-toed up the stairs searching for a bedroom. The place, on the whole, was very small. I could see that it had been built for either a single person or a couple, but it was certainly too small for a family. There was an empty box room at the top of the stairs; it didn't have any windows, and it looked unused. A cramped bathroom was next to it. A single toothbrush lay next to the sink. At the end of the short hall was a closed door. There was nothing left for it to be except a bedroom.

Confident now that no one else was in the house, I walked quickly down the hall and turned the door handle, pushing the door open until it hit the wall. I don't know exactly what I was expecting to see. Maybe more of the same monotony I'd witnessed in the rest of the house?

No. Instead, my fears were confirmed.

Placing one foot over the creaking threshold, I looked up at a wall plastered in pictures of me. I was dumbstruck.

The front door rattled open.

I heard Al downstairs. On the phone. He was having an argument. Again.

I stopped breathing and started to panic. I was in his room. Was he going to come up here? I willed him to leave, but the thudding footsteps up the stairs confirmed he was going to find me. I listened to his conversation. He was accusing someone of something, not doing their job maybe? I wasn't sure and didn't have time to figure it out. I had to concentrate.

Then, I remembered the New Year's party at home and how I walked completely unnoticed all the way to the kitchen. I thought about how I managed to do it, and about the times I'd practiced with Natasha in the living room, entering and leaving without her so much as looking up from her book. The fear fractured my concentration at first, splintering my thoughts. But as the footsteps neared, I managed to focus all my energy onto creating the silver, reflective sphere around me. I intentionally thickened it, so much so that I could barely see out.

I stood, clinging to Al's bedroom wall when he walked in. I saw his blurry arm lower his phone into his pocket as he sat and began to search through his desk. Finding nothing he was after, he stood up to move towards the dresser and stopped in front of me.

I could hear him breathing.

His out-of-focus silhouette turned to face me, pausing.

I felt he was listening for something. Me.

He abruptly turned and continued to rifle through drawers.

I desperately wanted to know what he was looking for, but all my attention had to be on maintaining my shield. The last thing I needed was to be alone with him right now. After an eternity, Al left again, clambering down the stairs and slamming the door shut behind him.

I breathed a huge sigh of relief, grateful that he hadn't noticed the lower lock was open when he returned. After a few minutes maintaining the bubble around me, I cut the cord of light between me and it, forcing the thick sheet to burst heavily and dissolve into the air. I was exhausted. Panting, I threw my hands up over my face and slid down the wall and onto the floor. My heart thumped loudly in my ears and, as it gradually slowed, I blinked through the gaps between my fingers. All I saw was me. Photos of me at the museum, walking to the shops, at the pub, each with scrawled notes over the top of them.

I felt sick.

My hands slid down over mouth, I stood up and looked closer, edging towards the wall. Half of the photos had been taken before I met Al in the wine bar—before I was even matched with him on the dating app. There was also a picture of a crystal. It must be the one Natasha found in my room, or one just like it. It was black with jagged edges. There were strange symbols marked over the picture of it that had been printed out and stuck to the wall. A photo of us all in the pub was central to this collage of obsession. I rested my fingertips over Rafael's face. He was laughing at something Natasha had said. His head was thrown back. Stroking the picture, I squeezed my eyes shut so they didn't tear up.

I glanced around the room and noticed the desk again. Papers with bullet-point plans scribbled frantically in pencil were strewn across it. He was pinpointing times when I would be by myself, times when nobody would expect to see me for a while. My shift schedule at the bookshop was there, too. At the top of the paper was a four-digit number, written in ink as if someone had traced over it several times. I recognised it immediately as my phone's pass code. He must have seen me put it in a million times when we were together.

My head was swimming. I had to assume Al knew everything about me, not just from how interested he seemed in me when we were together but from delving into my personal life and hacking into my mobile phone to snoop through texts and emails.

I had seen enough. Backing out of the room, I fled down the stairs, out of the front door and ran.

Waiting at St Pancras Station, I sipped nervously on a coffee and frenetically glanced up and down the platform. I was keeping an eye out for Amber and her girlfriend, but I was mostly worried someone was watching me. I took out my phone and went into the settings to change the pass code. Then, I searched for a VPN app to download and installed it onto my phone, both securing and encrypting my messages from now on. Finally, I went back into settings and disabled the 'Location Services' option. I wasn't a tech wizard, but I knew this would go some way to stopping enemies from getting into my phone or tracking me. It meant no one would be able to find me, even the police, but I was willing to take that risk. As I slid the device back into my coat, I heard Amber calling my name.

"Scar-Gar!" She shouted. Ever since Jennifer Lopez became "J-Lo," she'd loved to shorten my name in the same way. Even though it wasn't as catchy, she was sticking to it.

I stood up and waited for her to run over. Another girl behind her was sheepishly trying to keep up.

"Hey Bams. How are you?" We hugged tighter than usual. Maybe it was because of the honest conversation we had last time we met or because she knew there was an emergency I needed her for.

"Good, thanks." She turned to the short charcoal-haired girl behind her wearing black jeans and a beige trench coat. Her dark purple lipstick was bold but matched her outfit beautifully. I could see why my sister liked her. "This is Jessica."

"Hi, I'm Scarlett. It's nice to finally meet you!"

"Likewise. Bit mysterious, all this?"

"Oh, yeah. Sorry about that. Urgent situation and I need all the help I can get."

"Lead the way!" Amber cut in.

I turned and guided them to a nearby café. We sat down and ordered lunch before I got into the meat of why I had called them. "You're going to think I'm crazy." I took a sip of water, placed the glass back on the plastic table and looked up to guage their reactions.

"You mean more than normal?"

"Very funny."

"Just tell us what it is, Scarlett. You're making Jess think you're a drama queen."

"No, no, she's not!" Jessica piped up, obviously worried about offending me. I could tell she was a polite girl.

"Okay. Listen, I don't want to go into it too much, but I'm in trouble. Nothing I've done, but something bad might happen to me if I'm not careful."

Amber and Jessica sat wide-eyed, eyebrows raised, willing me to go on.

"So, tonight I have a plan that will help . . . hopefully." I leant in across the table and began to tell them in detail what I needed them to do for me that evening. I explained how we were going to do it and exactly how we were going to get away afterwards.

The girls drank in every word.

When I was finished, I sat back in my seat. The sandwiches we'd ordered set idly between us. I was terrified they would say no. They might even warn people what I was planning.

After a long silence, Jessica gently leant in, placed both her elbows on the table, and spoke. "Count me in," she smiled.

"Me, too," agreed Amber as she put her arm around Jessica to pull her in tight.

I sighed gratefully, and we laughed, dissipating the tension. The waitress brought over a pot to refill the coffees, and we sat in our booth chatting normally for a while. My appetite sprung back into action. I took a large bite of my sandwich and grabbed a few chips from the plate in the middle. Despite our impending mission, it felt important to catch up on the little things, so I took the opportunity to ask Jessica about herself.

"English," she mumbled through a mouthful of BLT. She cupped her hand under her chin to catch the crumbs.

"That's what I did!"

I caught Amber rolling her eyes. "I told you she would get excited."

"I'm always excited to meet a fellow literature lover." I beamed at them both.

"I also have two brothers," Jessica went on, "who are both are in the army."

"Didn't fancy it yourself?"

"Ha. No. I went through enough combat growing up with them."

"And where did you do that?" I asked, scooting along to get the ketchup within reach.

"Do what?"

"Grow up with them?"

"Oh . . . in Kent. I'm from a place called Maidstone. Nice enough. My mum is originally from Thailand though."

"That must be where you get your gorgeous hair from!" I had always wanted poker-straight hair. Jessica's looked like it was made of silk.

"Yeah. She came to the UK to look for work and met my dad. They were in the post office. Mum was sending a package home." Jessica turned to Amber with eyes that pleaded for an interruption to my barrage of questions. As a result, I got a sisterly kick under the table.

Looking at her again, properly now, I saw details that had escaped me at the train station. Jessica sat awkwardly with one leg hitched up onto the bench hugging her knee. A mole lay exotically to the side of her left eye, and her long hair flashed various shades of dark brown layered through the ends. I could feel the energy emanating from her; it was warm, comforting and good. I knew I could trust her.

That evening we travelled in silence. The familiar underground carriage seemed suspiciously muted, warped with my own fears and apprehensions. It was very late, nearly midnight, and I looked at my sister and her girlfriend sat opposite, both staring blindly at the ads posted above my head. They had agreed to help me unquestionably, a factor I had been relying on. I had considered telling Amber about my abilities, but I was only just getting used to them being real myself. How do I explain them to someone else when I didn't fully understand them? How would I even broach the subject? I had decided to tell them as little as possible and hoped they would trust me.

We arrived at our stop. I signalled it was time to get off. Everything was so familiar that I was almost on autopilot. The posters had changed, but everything else was where it had been, probably for decades. The smell of the corner shop heating up stale pasties breezed past. For a moment, I felt as though I was really going back to work. Again, I snapped my mind back to the present. We reached the last corner before the museum, bathed in the dim orange streetlight. Resting my hands on the cold brick wall, I peered across the road to make sure no one was around. Luckily, most of the businesses around there shut fairly early in the evening, and the lack of places to drink meant it was deserted.

Amber and Jessica stood behind me silently waiting for further instructions. I could hear them breathing, shuffling their feet on the pavement, nervously waiting for my signal. When the time was right, I gave it.

"Okay, now!" I whispered, looking at my watch.

They nodded and started casually walking towards the front door of the museum. They knew to look like tourists wanting to check the opening times on the door. Meanwhile, I rushed round the back to the main office window. I was counting on Jackie's inability to squeeze any money out of the budget to get it fixed. I rattled the latch loose, smiling as it dropped open. Worrying about the noise, I carefully slid the window up and climbed inside very slowly. My heart was beating fast. I could barely hear anything except the blood thundering through my veins.

Stopping to collect my thoughts, I reassured myself. *Relax. You know the alarm code.*

The office door was five feet away. As soon as I moved towards it, the alarm would go off. I would only have thirty seconds to turn it off, and it was located by the front door.

They change it every three weeks, increasing the last digit by one each time.

I looked around the office. The desk looked messy. I felt bad for Jackie. Her job must still be a nightmare trying to spread everyone so thin.

It's been eight weeks since you left, so the last digit has gone up by two.

Trying to concentrate, I thought back to the plan. Amber and Jessica would be waiting nervously at the front. I had to let them in. I repeated the new security code over and over in my head and leapt at the door.

A high-pitched tone cut through the air.

One . . . two . . . three . . .

There were 27-seconds left to get out of the office, run to the front door, and punch in the new code.

I grabbed the door handle to turn it and bolt out the office but was stopped.

It was locked.

I searched for a latch to turn. Nothing. I tried to unlock it with my palm, like I did with Al's front door, but I was frantic and couldn't focus. This was why I'd planned everything with as little magick as possible. I couldn't control it in times of stress, and for this I had to be in control.

The lock still wouldn't budge. Counting in my head the seconds until the alarm would go off, I looked around the room for a spare key but found nothing.

Eight . . . nine . . . ten . . .

I scolded myself for not remembering Jackie locked her office door at night. Of course, she did. I was an idiot! Looking back at the window, I thought about bailing on the plan, just letting the alarm go off and making a run for it, but I was already this far.

Twelve . . . thirteen . . . fourteen . . .

I closed my eyes and steadied my breathing. The mosquito-like whine of the security system faded away. I cleared my mind. The fear of getting caught, the guilt of breaking in, the excitement of what was to come—it all muted into nothing. I concentrated on the door with its flaking beige paint and scuff marks on the bottom. I looked down to the gold-coloured handle, chipped slightly at the end, and followed my eyes down to the lock. I could see straight through the black, key-shaped hole to the other side. The room was very still now, and I could feel the rusty contraption inside the door settled in its position.

CLICK.

I opened my eyes. The whining noise crept back into my ears. As my hand touched the handle the door flung open. I ran over to the alarm system box on the wall by the entrance and flung the plastic panel down to reveal the buttons. Steadily punching them in, I could see the countdown on screen.

Four . . . three . . . two . . .

The tone stopped.

I felt sick with relief.

Amber and Jessica were still by the door pretending to write down the opening hours when I unlocked the front door from the inside and let them in. Silently, we crept past the front desk and around into the cloakroom to talk.

"You remember what you have to do?" I asked, looking them each in the eyes.

"Yes, Scarlett. We went over it a hundred times." Amber was apprehensively shifting her weight from foot to foot.

"One hundred-and-one sounds like a good number to me," I said calmly. "What do you do now?"

"We follow the route you gave us to avoid the security guard. We go to the opposite wing to you and make a small noise. Then, when the guard comes to look into it, between us, we keep him busy, moving things, small things, just enough to keep him curious but not call anyone. After twenty minutes, we get out of there." Jessica recited my plan.

"Good. He won't know the alarm's been deactivated. It's only set to cover the lobby so that he can walk around the exhibits. Before we leave, I'll delete the security camera files from the computer in Jackie's office. Then we're done, okay?"

Jessica gasped and clutched at my sleeve. "The security guard. Won't he be in his office watching the camera feeds between rounds? He'll have seen us come in!" Her whispered voice was squeaking.

"That's why we came in exactly three minutes past the hour. I know his routine. He won't have been in his office. He'll have gone to the top floor and will start making his way down."

"What if we get caught?" Amber whispered forcefully.

I could tell they were nervous, but we had already gone over this. "You're a couple of girls who hid in the loos past closing time, who did no damage and didn't steal anything. Play dumb and they'll give you a warning at most."

They nodded. Peeking out from the cloakroom we were hiding in, we went our separate ways. Amber and Jessica headed to the art section, specifically the modern art exhibit in the north part of the museum, while

I followed my old routine path to the south. I breathed in the familiar smell and felt as if the last eight weeks had never happened. I was back at work, finishing a night shift before heading to the pub to see my friends.

So much had changed since then. Rafael was gone. Al had betrayed my trust, and I still had no idea what to think of Natasha. I felt myself starting to get emotional and stopped the train of thought before it distracted me too much. I reached the recognisable display and quietly stepped towards the centre of the room.

The Inca exhibit.

I could feel the power emanating from the cabinets already. I sensed myself even more attuned to the energy of the artefacts than I was before. The relics even glowed slightly, waves of colour drifting off them and dissolving into the air. I could feel my mind sharpen as I placed my hands on either side of the glass cabinet. The latches clicked open almost automatically. I lifted the lid.

Instantly, I felt it. I'd felt the presence the whole time I worked in the museum, but now it was so much stronger. A warm, accepting presence. A comfort that both soothed and energised me. The silky-surfaced tiger eye stones felt cool to the touch. I lifted them up to smell them, roll them around my fingers. I was getting lost.

The echoing sound of footsteps brought me back into focus. I felt a chill in the pit of my stomach. Had Amber and Jessica failed to keep the security guard from finishing his rounds? Had I been distracted for too long? I slid the stones into my pocket and replaced them with similar-looking cheap stones I'd bought from a holistic store. Quietly closing the lid of the cabinet, I silently crept to the opposite door from the approaching steps. I knew this place like it was my own home, so I could easily avoid the guard on my way out. But I had to go via the lobby to reactivate the alarm before leaving the same way I came in. Plus, I had to grab the security tapes on the way.

I checked the front door. It was unlocked, meaning Jessica and Amber had left already. I slowly turned the heavy latches, locking the top and bottom bolts and turned to the box on the wall. It was going to be tight, but it was the only way to finish this. I punched in the new code and set the alarm as I had watched Jackie do time and again at the end of a night shift.

The high-pitched whine started again. As quickly as I could, I ran back to the office. We had all been given a standard password for logging in to our accounts when we joined, I hoped that Jackie had never bothered changing it for the computer in the corner of the office. I had never seen her use it before. I steadied myself at the keyboard.

PASSWORD: "Art&Archeology"

Hardly uncrackable. Company passwords rarely were. A wave of relief rushed through me as the home screen appeared. The incessant whine continued around me.

Click . . . Click . . . Click . . . Click . . .

I had to wade through folders and subfolders to find this year, this month, this day, this evening, this hour.

There it was. One file covering the entire time we had been inside: *deleted.*

Nobody would ever realise it was missing. Nobody should ever need to look for it if they never realised anything was missing. I closed the various folders on the computer and slid the window open, climbing outside. As it clicked back shut, I heard the familiar sequence of beeps to indicate the alarm was set.

My heart was racing. Adrenaline was flooding rampantly through my veins. I panted heavily as I scurried away down a nearby dark pathway. Later, on entering the café where we'd agreed to meet, I burst with relief at seeing Amber and Jessica already there. I looked at their smiling faces and knew that there was no turning back now.

CHAPTER 13

A SHARP STREAM of sunlight broke through a gap in the curtains, greeting me brazenly when I awoke the next day. A note lay next to my bed on the nightstand in my sister's handwriting.

Had to get the early Megabus back to Loughborough. Thanks for showing me where you used to work.
Love Amber
(and Jess) xxx

They had slept in the living room on the sofa; students happy to sleep anywhere are easy to please. I slept in a bathtub once after a house-party. As usual, my sister was her low-maintenance, wonderful self. She was here when I needed her before shooting off back to her life again, no questions asked.

Rolling onto my back, I stared at the ceiling, thinking about my next move. Al had tried to call me a couple of times, as had the bookshop. I was sticking with the story about not feeling well. That bought me a few days to figure out my next move.

Callie noticed I was awake and padded her way up the bed. She had crafted a daily ritual of making chirping noises at me while pushing her little paw into my cheek until I got up and fed her. Her small round face was inches from mine now. Her miniature cat breaths wafting past my nose prompted me to roll over. After the rush of fear and excitement the night before, I felt like I needed a bit of normality. People who knew me couldn't start thinking anything was wrong.

I opened the Whatsapp group.

Pullin a sickie! ne1 up 4 lunch? — Me

Haha, yes! Midday? — Tash

Ace, George @ 12 — Me

See you there. — James

It was already gone ten o'clock. I could have a leisurely morning getting ready and then a nice shepherd's pie, or maybe a burger? I was starving. Wrenching myself out of bed, I went to have a long, hot shower. I was feeling good.

I went downstairs to feed Callie. Natasha had left for work already. Lucky for her she was one of the few people I knew who could still take an hour-long lunch break and not worry about her boss thinking badly of her. Most people I knew ate lunch at their desks, answering the phone and replying to emails, all between mouthfuls of sludge bought from the work canteen. In the kitchen, Callie sat expectantly next to her bowl, whining at me with a growing impatience for breakfast.

"Alright, alright madam!" I scraped her pungent food from the can and mashed it with a fork into her bowl. She reached up on her hind legs, her orange and white front paws mottled with black patches stretched up to my knee. "Here you go, Sweetie," I purred at her, placing the bowl on the floor and smiling as she busily chewed it down.

After a lazy morning routine of drying my hair, getting dressed and reading posts and articles on my phone, I grabbed the jacket I had thrown on the back of my bedroom door the night before and set off. The fresh air was a welcome shock to my lungs as I trotted down the front steps to the street. The bustling tourists were already in full force as was the wafting smell of street food creeping up my nose. With an empty stomach, I weaved my way up Portobello Road, dodging the antiquing couples who were peering curiously through windows and pointing at things they'll probably never buy. The music in my headphones was uplifting, and I swerved around the usual obstacles to the beat, taking it all in my stride. The medley of smells and sights and sounds muffled through my headphones reminded me of why I loved London. It was vibrant, energetic and the only place I'd want to live. Even with the hassle of rain and tube strikes it was all worth it for days like this. *Even with someone out to get me?* I thought, before pushing it from my mind.

Upon entering the pub, the same old scent of stale beer greeted me. I kind of liked it, except this time it was accompanied by a stab of heartache. Usually Rafael would be waiting at a table already. I searched the pub from the doorway and saw only Natasha.

"I'm the first one here." She shuffled up the bench so I could sit next to her.

I turned to give her a hug hello. It felt good. I missed her. With all that was going on in my life, I questioned who I could trust. Although I still wasn't entirely sure about Natasha, I was happy to go with my gut for now.

The menu was already open on the table meaning she was hungry. "Can I order?" She whined. "James isn't here. I haven't heard from him."

"Sure, okay. Order me lasagne, please! I'll message James in the meantime."

"Great. Oh, funny question for you—do we have a cat now?" Natasha was an animal lover. The smile on her face meant she was hoping for a "yes."

"Ha. That's Callie. She followed me home, and now I think I love her. Should have mentioned her to you! I never checked the tenancy rules though. I wonder if Ms Birch will mind if we have a pet?"

"Nah, who couldn't love that little face? Honestly, I thought I was imagining things last night when I heard meowing." Natasha was laughing as she got up to go to the bar.

I pulled the phone from my bag to hurry James along. I went to write *"James, your friends are hungry!"* but got distracted by the menu. My typing was clumsy and the phone autocorrected it all.

Named, tour fried are hugely!

I laughed at the nonsense. But before deleting it to try again, I paused. What was familiar about this? "Named" had come up instead of "James." It seemed so familiar. I searched through old text messages and found the one from Detective Inspector Locke. What had they found on Rafael's phone? Was it an unsent message?

I found the text and stared at the words Rafael had tried to send me.

Named I'd bit tour fried, ve fateful

Had he tried to text James? "Tour fried" was in both messages. I had tried to type "your friends." My mind struggled to unravel the accidental code. Rafael was trying to tell me something about James, and he'd mentioned him being my friend.

Why had he written "fateful?" It wasn't the kind of word Rafael would ever use, especially not in a text. I stared at the keypad on my phone. Hateful? Grateful? Maybe he hadn't meant for that "t" to be there. It was right next to the "r" and the "y." The "f" could have been a "c" if he'd overshot after the space bar . . . Did he mean to write "careful?"

Suddenly, I figured it out. Like when you see an anagram unscramble itself, revealing the answer.

"James is not your friend, be careful."

I panicked.

I looked around and was relieved to see Natasha still waiting to get the bartender's attention by waving the menu at him. I needed more time to think. I stared back at my text messages and saw one I couldn't remember sending her. Odd. I never texted her. We always Whatsapp'd. I opened it to see a message sent on the night I was attacked on Portobello Road. It told her I would be staying at Al's that evening, and she shouldn't expect me back. It was a message he must have written when he borrowed my phone.

On seeing Natasha handing over money at the bar, I grabbed my bag, went to the bathroom, locked myself in the cubicle and sat on the toilet lid. I needed space to make sense of this. Al had intended to stop Natasha from raising the alarm when I went missing. Why was Rafael trying to warn me about James? Had James killed him? This was absurd. Why on earth would he do that? He had no reason to hate him. No motive to want him gone . . . as far as I knew.

I racked my brain to figure it all out, but I was overwhelmed with a lack of air. The bathroom suddenly smelled rancid, the chemical air freshener adding to the suffocation. I needed clean air, and the windows were too small. Pulling open the door back to the pub, I saw the emergency exit next to me. It led to the back alley. I think staff used it as a shortcut to the bins. I leant my body weight against the metal bar to open the door and stumbled outside. My throat felt as if it was closing. Nausea was creeping upwards. I thought about yet another person I trusted being a part of who-knows-what and stepped dizzily down the passageway. Doubled-over, wary that I could be sick at any moment, I felt an ear-splitting, knife-like crack to the back of my head.

Then I felt nothing.

My eyes twitched open. I could smell dusty, dank surroundings, but I couldn't yet raise my head to look around. It felt like a needle was piercing the back of my skull. Everything hurt. Lifting my hand to the back of my head, I gingerly inspected the source of the pain with my fingers, raising them in front of me only to see a paste of dark red blood and black dust. I followed the stains up my sleeve. It wasn't long before I realized that I was covered in black, dusty smudges.

As I tried to sit up and shift my weight onto my elbow, I felt a hundred sharp bites on my palm, as if the floor was covered in glass. I could see that my wrist was bandaged. I didn't remember hurting it, although it still stung. I peeled off the white fabric and saw a recently stitched slit in my skin.

Eventually, after heaving myself upright, I looked about at the dirty brick walls. A single light bulb hung from the ceiling. It was the only thing keeping me from being in total darkness. Piles of black rocks were scattered around floor. They looked familiar. That must be where the dust was coming from. There was a steel-grey door five feet away from me that looked depressingly impenetrable. My only glimpse out of this room was the small, barred window in the door.

I wondered what was out there. My mind became clouded with questions as I started to remember. I could see myself getting ready in the morning. I fed Callie and went somewhere. Yes, I went for lunch, but I didn't remember having lunch. Why not?

As I began to unfurl the last day in my memory, I heard a noise. It was a rasping whine. The closer it got, the more it sounded like a distressed woman. As she approached my door, I could clearly hear her disorientated cry for help. My blood chilled. The confusion I'd felt until now turned to fear.

Rising cumbersomely to my feet, I stumbled to the door to try and see what was happening. I attempted to shout, but my voice got lost in my throat. All that came out was a gargle. I coughed and tried again. Projecting weakly, I asked if anyone was there. I saw through the narrow gaps in the bars the outline of a girl being dragged by her arm. She was small, reluctant and heavy. Her guard was having to do most of the work in transporting her. As she passed in front of my window, she looked up, and our eyes met for a moment. I only saw her for a split second. That was enough to see her distress, her hopelessness. I saw her trying with every ounce of strength to fight back but being almost completely incapacitated.

The sound of her pleas then dimmed until the hallway was silent again. I shuffled back into the room. Only it wasn't a room. I was in a cell, and I wasn't the only one. Other people were being kept here. Someone hadn't just taken me. They had imprisoned me. Why?

It took a couple of hours until I felt like I could look around my cell properly. The black rocks looked familiar. Al had a picture of something similar on the wall in his bedroom. I used the soles of my shoes to push them all to the opposite corner of the cell. I tried to sweep all the dust over to the pile I had created. And, as best I could, I brushed the black filth off me. It was in my hair and covered my coat and jeans. Going back to my corner, I already felt a bit clearer-headed, but not enough to be able to figure out what was going on. Everything still seemed dulled. I was tired. As the hours went on with nobody around, I gradually fell back asleep.

CLUNK!

The sound of a latch being dragged across the outside of the door awakened me. Groggy still, I heard muddled voices coming towards me. Then, I found myself being lifted up onto my feet. I stumbled and felt large hands grabbing me by the arm to keep me upright. It hurt, but my moans of protest were ignored. Reluctantly, I was led out of the cell. I lifted my head up to see what was around me; it was a similarly bleak-looking corridor. Passing other cells, I peered through the barred windows and saw the lonely outlines of other girls slumped in corners, covered in black dust.

We trudged along the passageway slowly. I could hear the voices getting impatient with me. They had harsh cockney accents and sounded like the kind of guys you find working the door of nightclubs. My feet dragged a little off the floor as I was half-walked, half-lifted by my burly escorts.

As soon as we arrived to wherever we were heading, I was dumped in a chair. In front of me was a woman at a desk. They chattered as I sat in pain three feet away from her. I inched my gaze upwards to see her face. The light in the room was brighter than the cell. My eyes hurt, but I could make out a few differences. This room wasn't dusty, and the desk looked expensive. There was gold lining around the red leather surface. The woman was writing quickly. I couldn't understand what was being said, but occasional words broke through.

"Level 5," said one man as the woman kept writing. "Potential for higher."

Her hands were pale with long fingers and talon-like nails painted red. I concentrated harder to listen to what was being said.

"Telepathy," mumbled the other man, followed quickly by something about "manipulation."

"Any divination?" The woman queried, her eyes still locked on the paper in front of her.

"None noted so far, but, as mentioned, there is potential."

"Right." She nodded.

"Telekinesis, too."

"Okay, thank you. I can tell she's in good condition. Take her back."

The woman's face was as pale as her fingers except it was powdery with makeup. Her high cheekbones were dusted with a light pink blush, and her stubby black lashes clumped with mascara framed her round eyes. She was dressed smartly, as if she worked in an office, and had an administrative air about her.

I could tell she was not on my side. She didn't even raise her eyes to look at me. Instead, she was only interested in what the men were telling her. In that moment, free of my cell with distracted guards, I wished I had an ounce of strength inside me to escape. I was fairly sure I could injure these two men enough to make a run for it, but I couldn't even muster my heavy body to its feet.

They dragged me back to my cell, and dumped me on the floor. I was alone again. I had no way of telling for how long. At one point, I was thrown a piece of bread. It landed a few feet away from me and rolled along the floor, collecting black specks on the way. I ate it, too hungry to worry about whether it was safe or not.

After what felt like a few hours later, I was abruptly awoken again, pulled up onto my feet and dragged the opposite way down the corridor by the same men. We started getting closer to a loud speaker. The voice coming over it was familiar. I realised it was the woman from the office earlier. She was reading a list of some kind. A low, electronic tone was sounding briefly during each pause. A muscular arm shot across my chest and stopped me short of a door at the end of the corridor.

One man's voice was directed at me this time. "Wait 'ere."

I didn't think I had many other choices considering the strength with which he was grabbing my arm. I started to think about what my options could be when he spoke again.

"Okay. Now. Go."

I didn't understand what he wanted me to do, so I paused. He suddenly opened the door and pushed me through it so hard that I stumbled to catch myself.

A bright spotlight shone directly at me, and my pupils contracted to pins. I lifted my arm up to shield myself from the blinding light when the woman's voice emanated from the loudspeaker again. She was repeating everything she'd written down earlier, but this time her voice was more soothing. She sounded inviting—sensual but formal at the same time.

I glared into the darkness around me, outside of the spotlight, and saw nothing. Then, I noticed something. Directly in front of me was the glare of reflection. There was a glass pane covering the whole wall, just like I had seen at the aquarium. I wondered what was on the other side and stepped forward for a closer look. The female voice changed slightly. She sounded less inviting now. Instead, her voice became more authoritative. I listened to her as she started announcing numbers.

"Four hundred . . ."

Except between each number was the now familiar low electronic tone.

"Four hundred and fifty . . ."

Each number was higher than the one before, but the tone remained the same. As I crept ahead to the glass wall, I felt an edge under the ball of my foot and realised I was stood on a platform.

"Five hundred . . ."

There was a deep chasm between the glass and me. I thought about it again. This wasn't a platform. I was on a stage.

"Five hundred and fifty . . ."

I wasn't trying to look *into* a glass cage. I was looking *out* of it.

The numbers continued to climb, and the tones kept sounding after each one until there was a prolonged silence. I listened hard.

"Nine hundred . . . thousand," the woman's voice announced.

Thousand? She carried on speaking, but I stopped listening. My attention was focused on nailing down what was going on. Someone had knocked me out and brought me to this place, put me in a cell covered in black dust, and paraded me in front of a strange woman. As I tried to untangle the last few hours, I was brutishly dragged back out the door and down another hall. I ended up in a different room this time. There was no dust in here, no crystals. It was smaller and nicer than the cell I had been kept in, with a less imposing door. There were no bars, and the dark-coloured wood looked expensive. I sat and tried to gather myself, going back to the last thing I could remember. As my mind became clearer, it started coming back. The text I tried to write to James, the message from Rafael, then going outside the pub . . .

I heard footsteps approaching from the hallway, followed by a loud click at the door. I expected the men to come in and haul me away again, so I pretended to be asleep. The door clicked shut again. I felt a hand on my shoulder. It was so gentle that I opened my eyes.

"Tash!"

She was crouching next to me, her mouth smiling, but her eyes lacked the same sparkle. "Scarlett, you're okay!" She leant over and gave me a hug.

I winced as she brushed the back of my head with her hand. "Kind of," I croaked. "What are you doing here?"

"Security is always much more relaxed after the auction. I couldn't get to you before."

"What?"

"Listen to me Scar. I can't help you get out of here. You have to do that yourself. Do you understand?"

I looked at her, struggling to make sense of anything. "Out of where?"

"They're going to put you in a car to take you away. Your owner won't have anything in the car to keep you weakened. They're too new to this, and the Company relies on you staying groggy until they get you back in a cell." Natasha was clearly desperate to leave. She kept checking over her shoulder to see if someone was coming.

My eyes drifted to the door to see if there was anyone there.

"Scarlett, pay attention to me! This is important! When you're in the car, that's when you need to figure out a way to escape. You'll need to focus. I know it's hard, and you're tired, but that's your only chance. Do you understand?"

"Get away . . . From the . . . Car?" It was all I could manage. The rest of Natasha's instructions were still processing through my weakened mind.

"Yes, Scar. Get away while you're in the car. I'll find you by the gates to the main road. By the gates out of here." Natasha pulled a vial of green liquid out of her jacket, held it up to my lips and tipped my head back. She poured the mixture into my mouth. "This will help, okay? This will take whatever you've got left inside of you and make it stronger. It's a temporary boost. It'll kick in by the time you get taken outside. Don't waste it!" She got up to leave and was about to open the door when she turned back to me. "I know you can do this. You're one of the strongest

I've met, and you don't even know it. Just remember to focus. Concentrate as hard as you can. You'll be fine." With that, she slipped back out the door.

Immediately, I wondered if I had hallucinated my friend. The sour taste in my mouth was a reminder that Natasha had given me something to drink. Something in a green vial. How on earth could she have got in here . . . and known about how to escape?

More footsteps approached. I shuffled back against the wall. The door swung open grandly this time, and the administration woman came in with a man. He was short, squat almost, with a comb-over to hide his balding head. I could smell his sickly cologne straight away and winced as he came to stand next to me.

"Why is she on the floor? Is she sick? I'm not buying her if she's faulty," he barked.

"No, Sir." The woman scurried over to him. "Not at all. She is weakened for your convenience right now. Do you have the handbook we gave you upon purchase?" She was grovelling. I could hear it in her voice. Her body language was equally pitiful, hunched over so as not to tower over him.

"Of course, I do. Does it say how to get her to do things? Does she know to obey?" He was kicking me with his foot. I nearly bit through my lip trying to restrain myself from thumping him. Not that I would have got very far, feeling as I did.

"As her master, you will be able to control her quite well, Sir. It's all in the handbook. Please do let us know if you have any further questions after you've read it." She gestured him back towards the door. "Now, if you would come with me to finish the paperwork, you can be on your way without delay."

The man grunted and strode back out into the hallway. She followed him and closed the door behind them. I heard the lock turn with a loud *clack*. Looking at the keyhole on my side of the door, I willed the latch to unlock like I had done so many times before, but it was useless. Any magick I tried to use was futile. Natasha was right. I was weakened.

The man was back before long, this time with a large, burly bodyguard. I was picked up and dragged limply outside to a waiting car. When I smelled the fresh air, I realised I was in the countryside. I saw trees and lawns. I looked behind me to see an enormous mansion. We had come out of a side door and straight to a line of expensive-looking cars. All of them had drivers patiently waiting for the boss to turn up. I was pushed into the backseat of a silver Bentley, alongside the security guard. I could smell the black leather seats, and the shiny wood panelled door slammed shut in my face. The short man from before got in the front seat and indicated to the driver to go.

Natasha's words started echoing in my head. *"Focus,"* she had said. *"Concentrate."* I had to think of a way to get out. I could feel the green drink taking effect, working it's way into my system. I felt stronger. Clearer.

The car wound its way down a very long private road. Looking out the window, I could see we were on a tree-lined driveway. I didn't have much time before we were out the front gate and onto the main road. What could I do? I continued looking sleepy while frantically trying to clear my head. Peering from the corner of my eye at my three fellow passengers, I noticed something. *No one was wearing a seatbelt.* Not the driver, the guard or the businessman. An idea formulated. Very slowly, I reached for my belt and slid it silently over myself and into the buckle, coughing slightly to cover the clicking noise. No one even looked round. I was cargo to them.

This was my chance. I was already starting to feel my mental fog lifting, so I closed my eyes and fixed my thoughts on the gas pedal. *Push!* The car started to speed up. I kept willing the pedal further towards the floor. The men were looking at the driver now, telling him to slow down, but they didn't know he couldn't. I could feel us racing down the driveway. The man in front was shouting and the driver was apologetically panicking. I opened my eyes to look briefly ahead out of the window. A solid old oak tree stood about fifty feet ahead of us. Carefully, I divided my mind between the pedal and the steering wheel, keeping the pressure on the gas while turning the wheel towards the tree.

"Slow down! What do you think you're doing?" The businessman's screeching voice twisted with rage. He reached with his stubby, fat fingers as he desperately tried to turn the wheel back. It wasn't budging.

"Sorry, Sir! I'm sorry! I don't know what's happening!" The driver had both hands off the wheel. Instead, his palms were pressed against his pale face, clutching at his cheeks with fear.

Right before the collision, I took a big breath in, pushed the accelerator harder and braced myself for impact.

CHAPTER
14

T HE BLINDING WHITE light dissolved slowly, and the gradual clamour of a horn grew louder. We were, all four of us, in a car wrapped around a large oak tree approximately thirty feet from the enormous gates at the edge of the property grounds. From what I could gather, I was the only one awake.

I crunched forward in my seat through broken glass to undo my seatbelt and look around. The hefty security guard to my left had been thrown forward with the weight of a wrecking ball. He had crushed the driver into the steering wheel and they both lay motionless. The seat in front of me was empty. It was only when I pulled the handle of the passenger door and kicked it outwards that I could see the short businessman stuck halfway through the windscreen. It was a brutal, bloody scene. The harrowing call of the horn was accompanied only by a constant hiss from the cracked radiator.

Stumbling backwards and breathing heavily, I remembered that I had to meet Natasha. Guilt started to creep into me as I saw the carnage I'd caused, but I reminded myself that I had to do whatever it took to avoid a life of imprisonment and slavery.

I looked down the driveway to the wrought iron gates: tall and black, adorned with golden accents. The way out of here. The way to freedom. I knew Natasha would be waiting, and I was desperate to get out of there. I yearned to go back to my normal life. To be in my little flat with a cup of tea on the sofa.

But I couldn't leave.

All those girls were still inside. Prisoners. Weak and powerless, just waiting for someone to take them away like they had tried to take me. I had waited so long to know if there were others like me. Now that I had found them, I couldn't leave them to be slaves.

I turned towards the house. It looked bigger from here. I could see the many floors and rooms, the historic-looking gables and at least a half-dozen chimneys. The first step was painful, but the bruising across my chest from the seatbelt was bearable. I had to get back there. Someone would soon realise there had been a crash. They were sure to drive past on their way out and see what happened. Then they'd be looking for me. Retreating away from the road and to the tree line, I tried to stay inconspicuous by creeping through the thickets and behind the large oak trunks up to the side of the house. I arrived to find the side door that we had exited still open, unsecured and unwatched.

I could walk right back in.

I stopped, hidden from view in the bushes, and sat on the ground with my head in my hands. What was I doing? These people had kidnapped me. They imprisoned me. They *sold* me! I didn't even know who "they" were. The woman on the loudspeaker? The men who marched me around? I would be walking in blind to a situation I was unprepared for against people I didn't know. Was I crazy? Maybe I should just go and find Natasha. She'd be waiting by the gate for me. We could leave. Then, I'd be safe.

The girl in the corridor flashed across my mind. She was so weak. I didn't want to think about where she might end up or who she might end up with. I didn't want to think about all the girls in the other cells. But I knew I had to. I had no choice.

Anger stirred in me. The people in charge of this sick circus were monsters who had no right to hold people like animals and auction them off for whatever rewards they would reap. I got to my feet to sneak over to the door. The wind blew a few strands of hair across my face, which I tucked behind my ear.

The door was still unmanned. Open. Inviting me back in.

Scanning my surroundings to make sure nobody would spot me, I bolted across the driveway and through the entrance, immediately diving around a corner for cover.

I heard voices. They sounded familiar. This whole scenario felt familiar.

I thought back to diving in the pub doorway on my way to work, waiting, obscured by the pillars. Al was about to walk past, that's why.

And that's whose voice it was.

I felt sick to my stomach. Every part of me wanted to talk to him, to try to clear it all up. I hadn't spoken with him in what felt like forever. I thought back to his house and his room plastered with pictures of me. His notes on my whereabouts pinned to the wall. I reminded myself he was an imposter. He had never been my boyfriend. He had used me. He had *spied* on me. To ultimately have me kidnapped. I thought about that night on Portobello Road. Why hadn't Al walked me home? Why had he said goodbye then immediately made a phone call? He must have been the one who tipped off my attacker that I was about to walk home alone that night. Everything that would have felt like paranoia before started to feel like an organised plot to get me.

The sound of Al's voice grew louder, and I realised he was suddenly around the corner from me. I could smell his cologne. It took me back to our first date in Gordon's Wine Bar. He'd looked so handsome. The candlelight had tinted the whole evening with a romantic glow. I had to fight the feelings of fondness that accompanied the image. Feelings of excitement, hope, and a sense of connection. It had all been a lie.

I had to start being proactive and take back control of the situation. Taking a deep breath, I concentrated on Al and tried to get inside his mind. His body was just a couple of feet away, so I focused on his thoughts and his consciousness. I found myself in a dark, cold, loveless space. But there was a distinct feeling of obedience, too. I could feel him receptive to orders. Maybe not from me, but he didn't know I was there.

"Hey, I have to go. I'll call you back."

Silence.

Again, he spoke. "Yeah it's me. I need to inspect a few of the units. Hold off the assessments for now. I'll let you know when I'm done."

I heard his footsteps start to fade away, so I peeked my head around the corner. He was walking toward the staircase.

There was a wooziness about this place, I could feel the effects of the black quartz in the basement, but its power was counteracted by the mixture Natasha had given me. I had to control myself, stay present and keep my mind focused.

Following him, I tried my best to create an invisibility shield around myself. A faint glimmer surrounded my body. I knew it wouldn't hold if someone decided to look straight at me, I wasn't strong enough. But I hoped to pass by unnoticed for as long as possible. Occasionally, I came across an open door, showing people milling about inside with drinks. The sound of chatter rose and fell as I passed. The hallways looked grand, nothing like the one that led to my cell. These were carpeted with a thick, red rug running down the middle. The walls were papered a rich, dark purple, punctuated with old-looking oil paintings framed in chunky gold-varnished wood. The portraits were mostly wealthy-looking old men. A couple of women's images were included in the collection, but they all had a nasty air about them. They were people who looked like they could buy and sell you in a heartbeat. A few wrinkled faces even looked familiar but . . .

Al suddenly stopped to enter a code into a keypad. He was stood next to a plain looking door, which beeped open to reveal a staircase. Hurrying through behind him as silently as possible, I saw him descend to the basement. I was back in more familiar territory: the smell of the dank air, the lack of light. I shuddered to be back here. The effects of black quartz hit me again, making me feel weak and confused. It was important to stay on track, otherwise I wouldn't be able to get Al to do what I wanted.

We walked a few more minutes along the cold, stone corridor and stopped in front of the first cell. He looked pained. Closing my eyes, I narrowed my thoughts down to a fine point, a point I placed directly in his head.

Open the door.

He raised his hand, and paused. His face distorted and his eyes pressed closed.

I forced the point harder into his head.

OPEN THE DOOR.

The lock clicked. He silently paced along to the next cell and repeated the same action. I willed him to keep going until all the cells were open. I communicated with him in the darkest way I could, knowing he would respond.

"Hello?" A weak voice emerged from the first cell. It was the girl I had seen dragged past my barred window earlier.

I was surprised she was still there. I opened the door quietly and crept inside. Despite my glimmering shield, she looked straight at me.

"Who are you?"

"Hi. I'm Scarlett." I smiled at her. The shining orb dissipated into the air as I broke concentration and approached the girl.

She was disorientated and expected everyone to be the enemy. I didn't want to scare her. Kneeling down beside her, I took her hand in mine. "You have to get out of here."

"Huh?" She stared blankly at me.

I helped her up to her feet, dusting the black quartz from her arms and out of her hair. "You have to get out of here. There is a door at the top of the staircase. Keep going down the corridor until you get outside. Then RUN." It was hard to be emphatic while whispering. Not entirely sure she was listening, I got up to check on Al. He was nearing the last cell at the end of the corridor. I briefly left the confused girl and crept up past him, looking inside the last cell to see it was empty. Perfect. Al began to mumble the words I placed in his head.

"This cell shouldn't be empty . . ."

"Someone should be in it . . ."

"I'm the only person here . . ."

Al was holding the door to the last cell open looking inside blankly. Leaving the key in the lock he slowly stepped inside and turned around to close the door.

Click.

Quickly, I snuck over to lock him in. For a moment, I looked through the barred window at the man I thought I'd fallen in love with. If I was going to get everyone out of this place, he had to be locked up. He was capable of things I never expected. Luckily he underestimated me too.

I turned around and spoke a bit louder to all the open doors. There had yet to be any movement.

"Everyone! If you can hear me, you need to leave! You are prisoners, but now the doors are open. You can escape. Please! Listen to me! You all need to get out!" I ran between cells looking in at the sleepy girls wearily lifting their heads at the sound of my voice.

One thing struck me again and again as I looked at their tortured, dirty faces. The same vivid, green eyes were staring back at me as if from a mirror. I tried to speak directly to their minds, but their mental fog was too thick, and I wasn't strong enough to get through.

A creak sounded from behind me. I turned to see the red-headed girl standing in the corridor. "Yes! Well done! What's your name?"

"Tabitha. Who are you?" She was more aware than the rest. Her words came out clearer.

"I'm Scarlett. Help me get the rest of the girls out. We don't have much time." I glanced up at the ceiling, realising there might be security cameras. Sure enough, two stared down at us from each end of the corridor. "Come on, between us we can get everyone out. They'll feel stronger once they're out of the cell, away from this dust."

One by one, we brought the girls out into the corridor and to the staircase. When we reached the top, I turned to them. "On the other side of this door is a long corridor. It twists and turns a bit, but there is an exit at the end. You need to run as fast as you can. Once you're free, you can hide behind the tree line and work your way down to the front gate. There will be a girl waiting called Natasha. She will help you."

Already, the girls were starting to awaken—still muddled but more alert.

I turned to Tabitha. "You seem strong. Make sure they get there."

"Okay," she mustered. "Thank you so much. We try and hide from Arania Corp, but they always find us." She seemed exhausted. Not just from today, but from life as a witch. A life of being hunted.

I wanted to ask her so many questions, but we had no time. As I hurried them through the door at the top of the stairs, I followed behind, making sure each one was ahead of me. Halfway down the corridor, I heard a cry. I stopped and spun around, trying to see where it came from. The girls continued to run in the right direction, except Tabitha who was pulling on my sleeve.

"Come on, we have to go!" She tugged at my jacket.

I pulled away. "There's someone else here. I can't leave someone behind."

I looked around. There were hallways off of hallways. I couldn't be certain where the scream had come from. I thought maybe it was someone who had been in the auction room instead of their cell. I had to find them.

"Come on!" Tabitha pleaded.

"No." I wrenched my arm from her grasp. "I'll be out soon. I can't leave someone behind to be a slave." I sprinted off in the other direction, following the sounds of the cries. As they got louder, I slowed down to determine which room the pleas for help were coming from.

I noticed the luxury that surrounded me: the crystal chandeliers that hung from every ceiling, the magnificent mahogany furniture, the floor-to-ceiling bookcases. I saw golden busts and china vases. £900,000 per witch would certainly fund a lifestyle like this. The portraits lining the halls seemed to watch me as I searched from room to room, getting closer to the pained wails echoing around me.

I was itching to escape, urgently wanting to run back down the hall and outside, when I came across a closed door. A big wooden door trapping whoever it was inside.

I took a deep breath. "You can do this, Scarlett."

The door creaked open.

I saw a room grander than any of the others. Not in size, but in splendour. A grand piano was poised in the corner, ready to play. The fireplace was adorned with expensive-looking items like Fabergé eggs, china vases and other antiques. A large writing desk made of dark— almost black-coloured—wood was in front of the window. Gold lamps lit its surface.

I couldn't see where the wails were coming from, but as soon as I stepped a foot over the threshold, they stopped. The cries didn't die down, or fade; they cut out like someone pressed "stop" on an audio tape.

I knew instantly I'd been tricked.

"I didn't think you were going to be this much of a problem, Scarlett."

The hair on the back of my neck stood up. I knew that voice.

Truth be told, I had been expecting that voice. But to finally come across it after everything that had happened was unnerving.

Mr Hopkins turned his chair slowly away from the window and towards me. The light from outside lit him from behind and made his face seem darker, more menacing.

"Mr Hopkins . . ." I meant for it to come out louder.

"Surely, you can call me Matthew by now?" He smiled a sickening smile. One of contempt. "You've caused a lot of trouble today, Scarlett. You've lost me a great deal of money. Lost me many customers." He was playing with a pen on his desk. I could tell he was trying to look casual, but there was something not quite right. He was angry but also nervous. Why?

"They've all gone." I announced proudly. "I helped them all escape. You'll never sell them now."

"My dear, do I look worried to you?" He sat casually, leant back in his expensive leather office chair. "See that incision on your wrist? You all have one. You're all easily tracked now. We can round those girls up in an afternoon, especially given the state they're in. They'll all be right back here in no time." The smile spreading across his face made me feel sick.

Had I not helped them at all?

I pressed on. "Who do you sell these girls to?" I wanted to buy time to think about how to escape, but I was also curious. "Why do you hunt us like animals and auction us off? Who are the buyers?"

"So many questions, Scarlett." Matthew got up out of the chair and walked around to the front of the desk. Leaning against it, he was still twirling the pen in his fingers. "You were a tricky one. Yes, you were certainly tricky." He laughed to himself. "We detected you a long time ago. It was faint, incidental, but last year, after your twenty-first birthday, you really flourished."

I had thought the same. Despite a life of odd occurrences and coincidences, it wasn't until I turned twenty-one that things seemed to make sense. "You've been watching me."

"Oh, yes."

"And following me."

"That was trickier. You assaulted the man I sent to take you, without even using any magick. That was impressive. It was difficult even after inserting people into your life to make it easier for us to catch you."

"James and Al?"

"Yes." Matthew smiled. "We knew you'd be quite taken with Al."

I remembered myself and asked again more forcefully. "Who do you sell these girls to? Why do you sell them?" I demanded loudly.

His face dropped. With narrowed eyes and a downturned mouth his voice darkened. "You, my girl, are an asset. A commodity. You are property. Properly controlled, you can reap vast wealth and rewards for someone. You can sway minds and opinions. You can foresee outcomes. If you weren't all such do-gooders, you'd be billionaires yourselves." Matthew's voice echoed with disgust. He looked down on me. "This club gives people who need those skills the chance to have them. Through you. Do you think tycoons just happen to know which deals will work? Do you think oligarchs just earn their power? There's a reason only a few rise to the very top. And you'd be surprised how much they'd pay for it."

"About £900,000?"

"Ah. Yes. Your buyer will not be happy you've disappeared from his control so quickly."

"I don't think he's too worried right now." I replied, realising that news of the crash had not yet reached the house. The lack of fear in my voice appeared to anger Matthew.

He dropped the pen and prowled slowly towards me. "You forget where you are, Scarlett. You forget *you* are now property. You are to serve someone else because they paid good money for you." His voice was a growl. He was close enough that I could feel his breath. It smelled like rancid oil and felt hot on my skin. "So go back to where you belong," he exhaled.

"No."

"What did you just say?" Matthew's pupils were dilated fully, turning his eyes black as he stared into mine.

"I said, *no*."

His bony fingers suddenly gripped my throat, pushing me back against the wall. The breath in my lungs got stuck—unable to escape, unable to pull in any fresh air.

His eyes were inches from mine, burning with hatred. He was finally showing his true self to me. "Who do you think you are? You're just another dumb witch, too stupid to know what to do with her own powers."

After a minute, he let go of my throat. I gasped for air. Pacing now, he turned to me. "Think about it! All of you! You're all capable of so much, yet we walk all over you. We keep you weak. We tell you what to do. And you do it! If you aren't strong enough to think for yourselves, then you don't deserve free thought." He was ranting now.

I thought about what he was telling me. This was an entire business based on harnessing the power of witches for profit, always selling to the highest bidder. These monsters willingly suppressed an entire group of people and kept them as their prisoners, and for what? Power, money, fame?

"Even if you were free," he was lost in his own ramblings now, "even if you could all think for yourselves, it would be dangerous. Who knows what you would do. Scorch the earth after a breakup? The public would be in danger. You're pathetic. You don't deserve the gift you were given."

"And you think *you* deserve it?"

Matthew looked up, almost surprised I was still there.

"Or maybe the buyers," I continued to ask him, "they are the good, generous people who *should* have had these powers bestowed upon them?"

"At least the buyers know what to do with them! Our members get somewhere. Achieve something. They make a name for themselves instead of fading into obscurity like the rest of the people on this planet." Matthew's words dripped with disgust.

I began inching towards the door. He was devolving into a rage, and I could feel the anger seeping out of his mind, infecting his whole body and the air around him. It looked like a thick mist, hazing the space around him, getting darker. I couldn't calm his thoughts. I couldn't raise a shield to stop him from seeing me. I just couldn't concentrate enough. The mixture Natasha had given me was wearing off. A few feet from the door, I felt his attention turn to me again. His voice was eerily calm.

"Scarlett, I think you are going to be too much of a problem for any buyer. Even the most experienced owner would have trouble with you, and you're far too knowledgeable now to be let back out into the real world. So, I'm afraid this is it." Matthew reached into his desk drawer and pulled out a very ornate knife. The engraved handle was silver. The blade was long and razor sharp. "Not much kills a witch, you know . . ." He turned the knife in his hand as he walked towards me. "Once they figure out how to harness their power, how to learn from ancient history and use their tricks . . . Yes, it's quite impossible to put them down. Once a witch realises her true strength, she falls out of our control. Luckily, we haven't let one get that far in a long time. I'm not about to let you break that streak, so this is the end for you, Scarlett."

Ancient history.

I couldn't believe my mind had been so hazy as to forget. I reached to unzip my coat pocket. Thankfully I had flung this on before heading to the pub that day. Matthew saw me reach for the zip on my pocket and lunged at me from across the room, loathsome murder in his eyes, the silver knife shining above me.

He plunged the blade into my shoulder.

I felt fire burning from the wound.

As he pulled the knife out, I saw the room spin. All I could hear was his laughing echoing in my head. Clutching at my shoulder with one hand, I dug the other into the lining of my pocket and found the tiger eye stones. They were warm, almost hot, to the touch. Taking them out, I quickly clenched them between my two palms, holding them, blood stained, up to my heart. They were searing hot now, but I felt no pain. In front of me, Matthew was revelling in the blood dripping from his knife, enjoying it drip from the point through his fingers and onto the expensive carpet. He soon decided to finish the job, grasping the handle firmly and hastening towards me.

I looked down at the white light shining from within my clasped hands. It felt good. I smiled as I raised my eyes at Matthew. He was frozen in place. Hanging mid-thrust, his arm was stretched out towards me. His eyes glowed an orange-brown, staring at my neck, and he was inches away from cutting my throat.

I slipped sideways, away from him, and thought about my position. I was stronger than he thought. The power from the stones was already seeping deeply into me, but I knew stopping time would leave me even more exhausted.

This was going to be close.

I let Matthew fall into the wall, stabbing his knife into the thick wallpaper and screeching in delight. The shock cut him short, and he turned to see me standing by his desk. Eyes widened, it took him a moment to realise what had happened. I looked down and noticed a security keypad linked to every camera in the building. There were multiple screens showing rooms all over the house. Each feed was watermarked with the name Arania Corp. Casually, I clicked the master switch off and turned to him.

"You're too late, Matthew." I smiled at him. "You should have hired someone who could finish the job that night on Portobello Road."

Again, he ran at me, screaming and driving the knife at my neck, but it was no use. I could evade him at every lunge with the briefest of time pauses. His lifetime of experience manipulating weak, inexperienced witches was no help to him now. He was exhausting himself with every roar, with every leap. Eventually, he collapsed on his knees.

"This needs to stop," I growled into his ear.

He was panting and blinking the sweat out from his eyes. "It'll never stop."

"It's GOING to stop." I held the knife, now in my possession, up against his throat. The point pressing against his pale skin. I looked behind his left ear and clearly saw the tattoo I'd noticed back in the bookshop. It was of a spider web. And it was identical to Al's tattoo.

"If you kill me," he whispered, "you'll never see your friend again."

"Natasha? She's already long gone."

"No. That idiot, James, didn't realise she was your chaperone. He thought it was the other one. The man." His voice was strained, but confident.

"Rafa?" I pulled the knife away from his neck.

"Yes." Matthew's thin lips spread into a grin. "If you switch the security cameras back on, you might see a familiar face."

Rushing over to the desk, I flipped the master switch and waited for each screen to flicker back to life. I saw empty cells, businessmen in waiting rooms, the strange woman with the wild black hair in her office, but I couldn't see Rafael. Not until the last camera feed. He was sat lifeless, staring at the wall, chained to the ground. Desperately looking for any information, I saw the feed was labelled LB2.

"What's LB2? Where is it?" I shouted, brandishing the knife now.

"I have no idea." Matthew was mocking me. He knew I couldn't kill him until Rafael was safe. I wasn't going to kill him anyway, but he didn't know that.

"Lower Basement? Is that it?" I tried not to beg or sound like I was pleading with this monster, but I had to find Rafael.

His flinch gave it away.

"That's it! There's a level below the basement?"

Matthew was still on his knees. I was confident now and strode over to him. He had a sickening smile on his face. I pressed the blade of the knife against his cheek and dragged it firmly over his skin down to his neck. Blood trickled slowly down his face. The smile faded into fear.

His eyes rigidly stared at mine. He changed tack. "This isn't you, Scarlett. You can't kill someone." His tone was superficially authoritative. Firm but with tell-tale cracks.

"Shut up." I had had enough of him telling me who I was and what I could do.

"Think of your parents. What would they say? What would your sister say?"

A smile crept across my face. I knew exactly what they'd say seeing me faced with this putrid excuse for a man. My dad's voice echoed his own father's words in my head.

Neutralise the threat. Any more and you're no better than the bad guy.

"What?" Matthew's eyes became wide with fear.

Stood in front of his pathetic form, I tucked the silver knife into my belt. I was never going to kill him. I couldn't. Even though he would easily have killed me.

Matthew started to laugh as he saw me putting the weapon away. He laughed harder, his voice manic like a hyena, as I walked past him to the door. His laughter stopped abruptly once the priceless vase crashed into the side of his head, knocking him unconscious to the floor. Dropping the ceramic chunk that remained intact in my hand, I left him lying in the study. Then, I ran to find my friend.

CHAPTER
15

H URTLING DOWN THE hallways, I searched for a lift as images of Rafael cycled through my head. I'd thought of his face so many times. Smiling. Laughing. I never thought I'd see that face again. Emotions began to bubble up, reaching my eyes and filling them to the brim. My friend was alive! On the monitor, he looked weak. His fragile body was cowered on the floor, but he was alive.

Occasionally, I had to dodge passing members, ducking and diving into empty rooms to avoid being spotted. I finally found a service lift and frantically stabbed at the down button until the doors pinged open.

3

2

1

G

B

LB

I had to go down into the deepest bowels of the house. My chances of getting out would be limited, but I had no choice. I had to save Rafael.

"I'm coming, Rafa. I'll get you out of here. Just hang on," I muttered to myself.

Waiting an eternity for the doors to ping back open, I heard a loud *clunk* when the lift stopped. The shiny silver doors separated to reveal a similar level to the one I had been held prisoner on. The smell of stagnant water hit me. As my eyes adjusted to the darkness, I realised that there wasn't much down here. Small scuttling noises pierced the silence now and then, but, otherwise, I could only hear the sound of my own shallow breaths.

I stepped forward with a mix of caution and eagerness, and made my way down another dimly lit corridor. Then, I came across an old, wooden chair. It was stationed next to the door of what appeared to be another cell. A couple of worn magazines and empty drink cans were on the floor.

I peered through the door's small, barred window and saw Rafael.

My heart both broke and leaped at the same time. I would have done anything to see Rafael again, but seeing him so feeble and damaged was a lot for me to take in. His grubby clothes had stained to the same grey as the stone floor. He was fading into his surroundings. There was only a glimmer of life.

"Rafa! Pssst! Rafa!"

He stirred briefly but remained largely in place.

"Hey! It's me, Scarlett! Remember me?" I was trying to think of anything that would nudge his memory and remind him of his real life. "Come on! Leeds University nights out? Pub dinners in The George?"

Slowly, he lifted his head. "Scar?" He croaked my name.

"Yes! Rafa, it's Scarlett! I'm here to get you out!"

I could see his face now. The thin light from the naked bulb hanging from the ceiling of his cell illuminated him enough for me to see a tear trickle down his dirty cheek.

"How did you . . . ?"

"I can explain everything." I looked quickly to either side of me. "But not now." Whoever was stationed outside his door would be back soon. I had to think fast. "Rafa, are you hurt? Can you walk?"

"I don't know." He shook his head. "I haven't tried in . . ." He faltered.

"Three months?" They probably had him in here since the day they took him. Anger swelled inside of me. But I had to push it aside in order to focus. Focusing was easier down here than up in the level where I had been held. Another look inside Rafael's cell told me why. There was no dust covering Rafael. The black quartz must only be in the cells reserved for witches. "Try to get up." I urged him. "We don't have a lot of time, and I need to get this door unlocked."

I retrieved a couple of the tiger eye stones from the museum from my pocket. Relieved again that I had had the foresight to need them, I held them between my palms and up to my face. Something in me had known I'd need them and had known I was in more trouble than I could have expected.

I felt the shiny smooth surfaces heat up. They started to shine brighter, and the bands of gold began to swirl. I could feel energy flowing from them. It would only be a few moments and Rafael would be out of his cell.

But I was distracted by approaching footsteps.

Concentrate, Scarlett! I heard the final sound of a heavy *clack* echoing from the door lock. *Almost there . . .*

"HEY!"

Spinning around, I saw James at the end of the corridor. So, *he* was tasked with guarding the cell. Probably as punishment after mistaking Rafael for my "guardian," or whatever it was called.

I kicked the door open and ran to heave my friend off the ground. His muscles were weak and there was little fight in him, but he managed to walk with some help. When we got outside the cell, James was attempting to call someone on the phone. Lucky for us, there was no reception this far down.

"James," I said forcefully. Rafael was still clinging onto my good shoulder. "Matthew isn't going to answer the phone. All the other girls have gone. It's over."

His gaze snapped up towards me. "You stupid . . . !" He lunged at me in a rage. Pure hatred glowed in his steel blue eyes. I was shocked to see him look at me this way. It was a stark contrast to the James I had known over the last year.

I pushed Rafael into the wall and out of the way of James's fist.

He missed and was sloppy enough to let me grab his wrist and twist it around behind his back.

"James," I whispered in his ear, his dirty blonde hair pressing into my face. "This is over. We are leaving and you can't stop us." Steadying myself against the wall, I raised my right leg and kicked him powerfully in the back, sending him forcefully to the ground. He landed skidding across the grey stone floor.

James lifted his head up, grunting with pain while catching his breath. "That's what you think!" He muttered angrily.

As I gave Rafael an arm to hold onto, I saw James crawling in the other direction. Before we turned the corner, I had just enough time to glimpse back and see James reach up the wall and hit a large, round, red button.

A wailing alarm began to sound.

We had run out of time.

I hurried Rafael back to the elevator, but the buttons wouldn't respond to my repeated bashing. The lights on the panel were dead. I spied a door that looked less heavy-duty than the others. Beyond it was a staircase lit in pale white light from a single line of fluorescent bulbs overhead.

With Rafael's weight pressing down on my uninjured shoulder, we trudged as fast as we could up the concrete stairs, the alarm still blaring loudly around us. We didn't even try to talk; it was pointless. The aim was clear. We had to get out.

After six agonising flights of stairs, we emerged out of the stairwell and staggered heavily to an exit.

It was locked.

Stumbling between hallways, we looked for more ways to get out. They were all locked. Even the emergency exits weren't budging.

"Rafa! I don't know what to do!" I had to shout in his ear to be heard over the ear-splitting alarm. "These doors are locked electronically! I can't open them!"

We were trapped.

The windows were too thick to smash through. We had to dive around corners to avoid being found by the security teams storming through the hallways trying to find us.

"I don't know what to do, Rafa!" I felt broken. Having come so far, done so much, and now we were stuck. I was certain my skills would be useless if they caught me again. I'd be stripped of my clothes—tiger-eye stones included—and thrown in a cell full of so much black quartz that I'd be comatose.

Frantically, I started searching for back doors or servants' entrances, but it was impossible to explore without getting caught. I clung to my friend. He was still weak but using every ounce of energy he had to keep going.

"Come on, Scar. There has to be a way!" He croaked into my ear, the wailing alarm almost completely drowning him out.

I had to stop and try to calm my mind. I needed to create some stillness amongst all the chaos.

That's when I felt them. I felt all of them.

"This way, Rafa!" I shouted as we limped together back to one of the larger studies I had seen on the ground floor.

"They'll find us!" He shouted in a whisper. His body tensed up against my side. He was reluctant to follow.

"It's okay, we'll have time." I was concentrating now. We had to get to the right room while staying out of sight.

"Scar, we looked in here. It's no use." He had given up. I loved him for making it this far, especially after spending months locked up with no space to move, no friends or family to comfort him.

"Trust me!" I winced as I squeezed him tighter with my supporting arm. The knife wound felt like fire consuming my shoulder.

We made it to the lavish study. I placed Rafael down onto the rich velvet, purple sofa. Closing the giant wooden door, I propped my back against the nearby bookcase and pushed, leveraging my legs against the wall and tipping it in front of the only entrance to the room.

I turned to the bay window. We had tried to smash through it already with the desk chair and a heavy bronze bust, but the glass was too thick. I couldn't manage it by myself.

"What do we do now? We can't just hide in here. They'll find us eventually, Scarlett. I love you for trying, but," he let out a long sigh, rubbing his eyes, "I made my peace a long time ago that I was probably going to die here." His skinny frame lay slumped on the sofa. His grubby face stared towards the ground.

I sat next to him and placed my hand on his head. "I told you to trust me." I smiled and stroked his hair gently to ease his fear. "We're not in this alone."

I reached down to the floor and grasped the edge of the thick rug that covered the wooden floorboards of the study and pulled it towards me.

They were waiting, ready. I could feel them.

I looked up and across the room through the window. Standing in a row on the lush green lawn was every girl I had just released. Holding hands. They had come back to help us. Natasha was there, too. Her face was too far to determine an expression, but I could sense her nervousness.

"Help me hold this up." I instructed Rafael, pulling the heavy rug up over our knees.

"What? Why?"

"You'll need it in a second. I'll tell you when." I detected the churning of power. It was like an electric storm, and every girl was a separate lightning strike. The wind picked up outside, and I could see their hair and clothes blowing vigorously in all directions. The skies darkened as clouds rolled across, summoned by the combined spirit of these girls.

In the background, the alarm continued to blare. I could hear shouting coming down the corridor. My head spun towards the door to see the bookcase moving rhythmically, as if it was being pounded from the other side. Books were falling from the shelves, making it lighter and easier to move with each push.

There wasn't a lot of time left.

I joined the girls as I tapped into their passion and power, detecting their pattern of energy and slotting myself in to boost their strength. Like a hundred threads combining to make a rope, we merged our minds until it was too much for the house to bear.

"NOW!" I shouted at Rafael.

He helped me pull the rug up over our heads to protect ourselves. The thick window burst spectacularly. Shards of glass flew everywhere. Stabbing into walls. Plunging into the furniture. Bouncing off the ceiling. I felt cool air flood into the room.

Kicking the rug off onto the floor, I turned to pull Rafael up to his feet. His face was white. I remembered he had no idea why he was here, but there was no time to explain now. The bookcase was nearly tipping onto its front, the remaining heavy books struggling to weigh it down against the ramming from the other side. I hauled Rafael over to the bay window. We climbed through the shattered frame and jumped down onto the lawn.

Natasha burst into tears. Rushing towards us, she threw her arms around Rafael, squeezing him and crying. "Rafa! What are you doing here? We thought you were dead!"

"Not quite." He recoiled slightly in pain from her enthusiasm.

"Oh, sorry!" She stepped back to look at his face. "I can't believe it's you. We had a funeral for you. Did you know that?" She hugged him again until I pulled her away.

"I can't believe you did this." I gestured back to the window, the blustery gale still whirling around us.

"The girls! They didn't want to leave you. *I* didn't want to leave you! I gave them all some of the amplifier. They were weak but it was enough so that, together, we could do it."

I looked over her shoulder. They were all clearly eager to get as far away from this place as possible.

A familiar face stepped forward. "That was some good stuff your friend gave us!" Tabitha was smiling, holding her red hair from her face against the wind.

"Tabitha! Thank you so much for coming back."

"You can call me Tabby." She smiled. I could see the gratitude in her eyes. I hoped she could see it mine, too.

I wanted to thank all the girls, but Natasha had other ideas. "We need to go NOW," she urged. "I rang ahead for transport. I thought I was only taking you on my bike, but I think we'll need something a bit bigger!" She explained her plan as we made our way down to the iron gates, safely ensconced in the tree line. "The Council has sent reinforcements."

Gradually, we all poured out of the gate onto the country road leading past the entrance to the driveway. Lined up along the grass embankment were five cars. Piling into them all, we set off. After the last of us had run through the gates, Natasha locked them with the chain and padlock from her motorbike.

I turned to her as she climbed in one of the cars next to Rafael and me. "They'll know we're gone. What if they chase us?" The seatbelt stung against my bruise from the earlier crash as I turned to look out the window. I flinched back into place, looking down at the dried blood on my shoulder.

"You're okay now, Scar." She patted my hand. "You've done so much more than we ever expected."

"We?"

"Try and rest for now. You've been through a lot." Natasha turned to Rafael and smiled. "You, too."

"One more thing, Tash." I rubbed my forehead, worried. "Callie. Have you been feeding her?"

Natasha laughed. "Of all the things to worry about! Yes. She's got a rotation of people dropping in to feed and play with her. They even argued about who got to go first." She squeezed my hand tightly. "It was impressive she found you. I heard familiars naturally gravitate towards their witches."

My eyelids were heavy and I rested my head back on the seat. A combination of exhaustion and the come-down from the adrenaline ushered me to sleep before I could ask what she was talking about. When I awoke, we were in central London, pulling into a side street somewhere near Oxford Circus.

"Follow me." Natasha helped me out of the car as I was still groggy. She steered us both to an arch in a nearby wall. The red brick entry disappeared down a staircase.

"We're nearly there. The rest will follow us."

Rafael limped alongside. After some food and water in the car, he was already looking better. Stairs followed more stairs. Then, we boarded an old industrial lift.

We were going deeper and deeper under the streets of London. Still, Natasha wouldn't tell me anything.

"You'll see." She said, squeezing my hand.

Eventually, we came to an open area—a hall that looked as if it hadn't been used in a hundred years. There were people everywhere. It reminded me of a busy newsroom with people focussed on their laptops, headphones plugged in. Meetings were taking place around desks. It all looked surreal.

"What is this place?" I began but was stopped from asking any more questions by the chic, elegant figure walking over to me. "Ms Birch!"

"I told you to call me Ivy, dear." She smiled warmly and took my hand in hers.

The last person I expected to greet us was my landlady.

"Welcome! We've been so looking forward to welcoming you here. I see you've brought some extras?" She brushed Rafael's face with the back of her hand, he had just enough energy to blush.

"It's you behind all this?" There was something different about her, though. Before she could answer it clicked. "Your eyes? They're green!"

"Oh, yes. It's called a Glamour Spell, dear. The magick hides their true colour. Sadly, our greatest feature is also our greatest giveaway." Her face looked relieved to see me, but her smile fell after glancing at the knife wound in my shoulder.

"Where are we?" I asked again, looking up at the high, tiled ceiling. Originally white, time and water damage had stained it a dull grey colour.

"This," Ivy waved her arm as if to present it to me, "is the British Museum Underground Station."

"The . . . What? There's no station with that name."

"Not anymore, dear. But there was. Up until 1900 exactly, when it was closed forever. It's between Holborn and Tottenham Court Road Station. Used as an air raid shelter during the war. We started using it as our headquarters after that. Shame it's not nicer down here but quite fitting that it's underground." Ivy winked at me. "For now."

As I looked closer, I could see the resemblance to other Central Line stations.

Ivy turned away from me and towards Natasha. "Darling, you did a wonderful job. I've notified your team leader about your spectacular commitment as a chaperone."

"What's a 'chaperone'?" I was starting to see a pattern. Every time one question was answered another one cropped up in its place.

"Natasha here is a member of our Preservation Team. It was her job to look after you and monitor your progress into the world of magick."

I looked from Ivy to Natasha, who nodded in agreement. "That explains the mysterious notebook then." I jokingly poked Natasha in the arm.

"I didn't expect for you to . . . I mean . . ." She looked horrified.

"It's okay, Tash." I turned back to Ivy. "So you've been watching me all along?"

"Oh, yes, we've been looking after you as you found your feet. After that nasty break-in, I had some of the Council members create a protective shield for your home." Ivy turned me towards the back of the hall, and we walked slowly. Rafael and Natasha followed behind.

"That's why Al never came in the flat?" I turned, whispering to Natasha who nodded back at me. I straightened up again, not wanting to be rude. I had yet another question burning to be asked. "Ivy, what is this 'Council' you keep referring to?"

"Why, the Emerald Council, dear! We are the leaders of our community. We have been for centuries. Ever since that unfortunate year in Salem, we decided witches everywhere needed support. Here in the UK, we are very proud of our members, but we are a long way from where we want to be: living safely and openly among the general public. Arania Corp has pushed our people underground for centuries. The likes of Matthew Hopkins and those before him have tried to bury us many times. Little did they know our ancestors were the seeds of a stronger future for witches. We may only be saplings now, but soon we will join the forest as noble oaks."

"How did you know about me?"

Her sparking green eyes lit up, and she became nostalgic. "We can sense when a witch is born. Someone with a light inside them and the power to understand the world is easy for us to see. But not everyone chooses this life. Some continue their existence as a mere bystander of their abilities, being the victim of their incidental incantations. They never look any farther. But sometimes, every few years, we find a girl who cannot help but grow her powers. When you turned twenty-one, you noticed a change, yes?"

"I did." I replied, keen to hear every word she had to say.

"We call that 'Magickal Maturity' in our world. It is when you are fully formed in both your physical abilities as well as your magickal strengths."

Eventually, she led us to the back of the hall and into a small office-like room. "Natasha, take the lovely Rafael here to our healers. They will fix him up in no time."

They obliged, and I was left alone with Ivy.

There was a spookiness about the old office we were in. No natural light. Hidden away from the world. The fluorescent light gave it the look of an abandoned hospital. I could feel a history here; it had a bustling atmosphere until suddenly there was nothing. I felt a residual sadness. Or was it fear? I pulled the silver knife out from its place on my belt and placed it on the table.

Ivy beckoned a young man in to take it away. He did so with gloves on.

As I settled into my chair, the people shuffling around in the main hall caught my eye again. "Who is everyone out there? Are they all witches?"

"Many are low-level witches. Born with power but not enough to be in the field. We never want to put anyone in danger."

"And what are they doing?"

"Helping, dear. Where you were today, in the hands of the Arania Corporation," she paused to collect herself. "You were in the dragon's lair. Had you been transported, who knows if we would have ever found you again." She stopped again, taking a breath before looking up at me. "Every member of our organisation has one mission. To stop the trafficking of witches. Every person you see out there is following paper trails, finding auction houses, doing whatever they can so that our field agents have the information they need to save as many witches as possible. But it isn't easy. They evade us." Ivy began to speak as though she was talking only to herself. Her voice hardened. "It seems as though for too long we have been teaching witches how to protect themselves against the likes of the Arania Corp. It was reactionary and born out of desperation. Now it's time to take control of the situation. We need to stop the threat, not prepare the victims."

Suddenly, I recalled something Matthew had said. "We're tagged! I just remembered. They tagged us with a GPS tracker or something. I have a scar on my wrist." I held it up to show her.

Ivy shook her head sadly. "Yes. We're hunted, Scarlett. They treat us no better than animals that can serve their greedy indulgences. Don't worry. We know how to remove the tags."

"Why didn't Natasha try to save the other girls?" I asked, confused as to how she could have come only for me.

"Oh," Ivy smiled. "We knew you wouldn't let that happen."

This was so much to take in.

"Once we realised you had the tiger eye stones from the museum," Ivy leant forward, smirking, "- we should return those, by the way—we knew you would have the strength to get through the ordeal, despite a lack of formal training. I'm impressed that you intuitively knew how to empower yourself. It is, however, important to remember one thing."

Ivy sat forward in her chair. Her hands clasped together, resting on the cold steel desk.

"With training, you will soon be a force to be reckoned with, but do not become complacent. Witches before you have fallen because they considered themselves too powerful to be in danger. Simply being a witch puts you in danger. However advanced, however strong you think you are, they will never stop hunting you. Not unless we can change the way the world thinks. Not until we are all truly free."

I sat back in my chair and tried to sort through all the new information from the last few hours, but Ivy interrupted my thoughts.

We have been waiting for you, Scarlett. There's a reason you're sitting here with me today.

I looked up, surprised to see Ivy's purple painted lips gently resting shut. I waited to hear more.

Only a few of us are strong enough to take them down. Together we will stop Arania Corp. Stop them from tracking and kidnapping witches. From imprisoning them. From selling them into a life of slavery. The work you do here will be the most important work of your life.

This was the first time I had been on the receiving end of this kind of communication. Ivy's words felt warm and comfortable in my head. It was as if she belonged there.

In that instant, my decision was made.

It was clear why I had been led to Ivy and the Emerald Council, to all the witches fighting for the freedom of other witches.

I nodded my head and rose to my feet. Leaning both hands on the old metal desk between us, illuminated by the pale fluorescent light above, our shining green eyes met. I asked the only question I had left.

"How do we stop them?"

ACKNOWLEDGEMENTS

I would like to express my gratitude to the many people who saw me through this book—to all those who provided support, talked things over, proofread and offered comments.

I'd like to thank my editor, Lorna from Early Girl Publishing. We got there in the end and this book wouldn't be half as wonderful to read if it weren't for you.

Peter at Bespoke Book Covers did an amazing job with the cover despite constant suggestions for changes. You were very patient and the results were perfect.

To my husband, Charlie, who listened to me struggle for ideas, and who kindly let me hammer out my own thoughts by rejecting his. You supported me throughout this process, and without that support this book would not exist.

I have to acknowledge my own little rescue calico, Lucy, who would sit and stare at me while I tapped away on my keyboard. She has no idea she has been immortalised in print as Scarlett's familiar.

My parents, Stephen and Chelo, and my parents-in-law, John and Linda, your words of encouragement kept me excited about the finished product. I must also mention my godfather, Roger Moore, who let me live in his house when I first penned the rough outline of this book. It was a beautiful setting in which to create this world.

Finally, I must acknowledge my brother Chris, my friends, my neighbours, and anyone else who listened to me endlessly go on about subtext and themes.

ABOUT THE AUTHOR

S D C Forster is a British author. After living internationally in Asia and Europe she has now set roots down in the Middle East for the foreseeable future. Despite a technical career in broadcasting Forster often wrote short stories without ever submitting them. After taking the plunge to pen an entire novel she now has her eyes set on the sequel.